Bisc

Made in Savannah

Cozy Mystery Series Book 24

Hope Callaghan

hopecallaghan.com

Visit my website for new releases and special offers: hopecallaghan.com

CONTENTS

Cast of Characters

Carlita Garlucci-Taylor. The widow of a mafia "made" man, Carlita promised her husband on his deathbed to get their sons out of the "family" business, so she moves from New York to the historic city of Savannah, Georgia. But escaping the "family" isn't as easy as she hoped it would be, and trouble follows Carlita to her new home.

Mercedes Garlucci. Carlita's daughter and the first to move to Savannah with her mother. As a writer, Mercedes has a knack for finding mysteries and adventure and dragging her mother along for the ride.

Vincent Garlucci, Jr. Carlita's oldest son and a younger version of his father, Vinnie, is deeply entrenched in the "family" business and not interested in leaving New Jersey for the Deep South.

Tony Garlucci. Carlita's middle son and the second to follow his mother to Savannah. Tony is protective of both his mother and his sister, which is a good thing since the female Garluccis are always in some sort of predicament.

Paulie Garlucci. Carlita's youngest son. Mayor of the small town of Clifton Falls, New York, Paulie never joined the "family" business and is content to live his life with his wife and young children away from a life of crime. His wife, Gina, rules the family household with an iron fist.

Chapter 1

"This is a great night." Mercedes clapped her hands, doing a little side shimmy and bumping hips with her friend, Autumn Winter, as they grooved to Cool Bones and the Jazz Bands' opening number.

Cool Bones, a family friend and tenant of the Garlucci family, had been traveling for several weeks, celebrating the honorary distinction of being selected Georgia Jazz Music's recipient of the year.

To celebrate, the band was back home, playing where they'd gotten their start—at the Thirsty Crow in downtown Savannah.

During a break in the set, Mercedes darted to the stage. She gave Cool Bones a warm hug. "We're glad you're back home. We've missed you."

"And I've missed all of you." Cool Bones returned the hug. Autumn, also a tenant, slipped in next to her.

"Hey, neighbor. Thank you for keeping an eye on my place."

"You're welcome," Autumn said. "Mercedes and I made sure your plants didn't die."

"I appreciate you taking good care of them. Me 'n the boys are gonna stay put for a while now. All this fame and recognition is exhausting."

"I'm sure being recognized as one of the best jazz bands of all times is hard work," Mercedes teased. "As soon as you're settled, I'm throwing a party down in the courtyard."

Cool Bones waved dismissively. "I appreciate the offer, but you don't have to."

"I want to," she insisted. "I can't count how many times you've offered to play for me and my friends for free."

"We'll bring the music. How's that?"

"You have yourself a deal." She gave him a thumbs up.

Cool Bones returned to the stage while Mercedes and Autumn swung by the bar to order drinks.

The place was jam-packed. The band's recent award, announced on news channels and in the papers, had created an air of excitement. Locals were eager to help them celebrate, and Mercedes couldn't have been prouder of her neighbor and friend.

Steve, Autumn's brother, and his girlfriend Paisley arrived, crowding around the table. Carlita, Pete, Tony, Shelby, Elvira, her sister Dernice, and Luigi hit the dance floor, kicking up their heels to the tunes they'd heard so many times when Cool Bones practiced in his apartment.

During the next break, Carlita and Pete called it a night, once again congratulating the jazz band on their distinguished award before leaving.

The hour grew late, and the crowd thinned while the band finished performing their final set. Mercedes, Autumn, Elvira, Dernice and Luigi were among the last still hanging out.

"I'm gonna run to the restroom before we head home." Mercedes hopped off the barstool, making a beeline for the bathroom. She took care of business, washed her hands, and checked her reflection in the mirror above the sink.

Mercedes ran her fingers through her jet black hair before tossing the crumpled paper towel in the trash on her way out. Easing the door open to make sure no one was on the other side, she made a beeline for her friends.

Out of nowhere, the bar's entrance doors flew open. Flashes of black. Badges. Loud voices. Mercedes stood paralyzed as a small army of police officers cut through the center of the bar, all bearing down on Cool Bones and the band, who were still on stage.

Mercedes held her breath, watching in horror as an officer grasped Cool Bones' arm. He spun him around and began reading him his rights while he slapped a pair of handcuffs on his wrists.

The stunned onlookers moved out of the way, making room for Cool Bones. Flanked by an officer on each side, they hustled him toward the exit.

"BOO." The crowd started booing and chanting. "Let him go. Let him go."

Mercedes stumbled back, colliding with a table full of beer bottles. An empty bottle teetered and started to fall over. Lunging forward, she grabbed hold of it.

Crack. Mercedes instinctively ducked at what sounded like gunfire. She narrowly missed being struck by a glass bottle whizzing by her head. The airborne bottle flew forward, whacking an officer in the back of the head.

He spun around, a look of fury on his face. Mercedes, still holding the beer bottle she'd knocked over, carefully set it on the table. It was too late. The cop had noticed the bottle in her hand.

He strode over and grabbed hold of her arm. "You hit me with a beer bottle."

"I...I didn't. I swear. I bumped the table and knocked an empty bottle over. I grabbed it before it hit the floor. Next thing I know, I felt something whiz by my head. I ducked, and it hit you instead," Mercedes explained.

"Did you see her throw the bottle?" the cop asked a man standing only a few feet away.

"No." He shrugged. "I saw a bottle in her hand and then you got hit."

"I swear. I didn't throw a bottle at you," Mercedes insisted.

"You're lying." The cop unhooked his handcuffs and snapped them on her wrists. "You're under arrest for assaulting a police officer."

Chapter 2

"Hold up." Elvira stepped in front of the cop, blocking his path. "I know for a fact Mercedes Garlucci was in the restroom, which means there's no way she could've tossed the beer bottle at you."

"You need to get your eyesight checked. When I turned around, she was holding a bottle and looking right at me."

"Because it whizzed past my head. I ducked. You got hit. End of story," Mercedes said.

"Did you see her throw the bottle?"

"I didn't have to." The cop's eyes flashed with anger. "Step aside."

Elvira pretended not to hear. "You should take a look at the bar's surveillance recordings. I'm sure you'll find you have the wrong person."

The cop pushed Elvira aside. "I plan to. In the meantime, Ms. Garlucci can have a seat in the back of my patrol car."

Elvira trailed behind them. "You better be one hundred percent sure because she can sue you for false arrest."

"Elvira." Mercedes shook her head. Something told her the veiled threat wouldn't help the situation. "As soon as he sees the video cameras, he'll know it wasn't me."

"I suggest you beat it before I find a reason to arrest you too," he warned.

"Arrest me?" Elvira squared her shoulders. "I didn't do anything."

"You're harassing me and impeding an investigation."

"That's a crock." Elvira placed her hands on her hips. "I'm the one who suggested you view the surveillance cameras, a reasonable suggestion you should have thought of yourself."

Mercedes knew the exact moment her neighbor's snarky comment crossed the line by the look on the cop's face. Without saying another word, he placed her in the back of his patrol car.

He grabbed another set of handcuffs from his glove box and cuffed Elvira.

"What are you doing?"

"Getting a blabbermouth nuisance out of my hair."

"Y-you can't arrest me," Elvira stammered. "I wasn't anywhere near the incident. I was on the other side of the bar."

"Which is where you should have stayed." Mr. Aggravated Officer read both women their rights before shoving Elvira down on the seat and slamming the door.

Through the side window, Mercedes watched him walk over to another cop. He motioned in their direction before heading back inside.

"Great. Here I was trying to help you out and now I'm in the same boat," Elvira grumbled.

"It was a no-win situation, I'm afraid." Mercedes shifted to a slightly more comfortable position. "I wonder what happened to Cool Bones."

"The cops swarmed the place like they were taking down a terrorist." Elvira winced. "The jerk put the cuffs on too tight. They're pinching my skin."

"I'm sorry you got involved," Mercedes apologized. "This is all a huge misunderstanding. As soon as he finds out I wasn't the person who threw the bottle, he'll let us go."

"The bar has crappy lighting. There was a lot of action, which means there's a chance the cameras didn't catch the person who clunked him in the head."

"If not, I'll have to give Tony a call to bail me out."

"Ack." Elvira made a honking sound. "Not gonna happen."

"Why not?"

"It's the weekend. The cops can hold you for up to 72 hours. You'll be sitting in a cell until you can go before a judge. Based on my past experience, this won't happen until Monday. Assaulting an officer is a serious offense."

Mercedes' eyes widened. "Locked up all weekend?"

"I've been in the holding area of the downtown jail. It ain't pretty and it smells disgusting."

"Unfortunately, so have I. I don't remember it being awful, but then it passed by in a blur." Mercedes bit her lower lip. "Maybe Sam can pull some strings."

"On-again, off-again boyfriend Sam?" Elvira asked. "I thought you two were off again."

"We're kinda back on. I'm sure he can help." Mercedes grew quiet, mulling over their predicament. If Elvira claimed the jail was rough, it was probably ten times worse.

Long moments passed. One by one, the officers returned to their vehicles and drove off. Luigi, Dernice and Autumn appeared. Luigi was the first to notice them. He glanced over his shoulder and strolled to the back of the cop car.

Dernice joined him and began motioning with her hands.

Elvira struggled to read their lips. "What are they saying?"

"I don't know," Mercedes said. "I can't hear. These cop car windows are airtight."

"Consisting of ballistic glass or bulletproof windows in layman's terms. They're well sealed, by design, making it hard to hear," Elvira said.

"Where's the door handle?" Mercedes twisted to the side, fumbling for the door handle.

Elvira snorted. "There aren't any door handles in the back of a cop car."

The officer who had arrested them reappeared. He strolled over and had a word with their friends, who were still standing nearby.

Luigi motioned to them and then toward the building. All the while, the cop shook his head. Finally, reluctantly, they left.

"Uh-oh," Mercedes said. "They're leaving. Not a good sign."

"Nope."

The cop opened the driver's side door and climbed in.

"Well?" Elvira asked. "You're gonna let us go, right?"

"The video cameras show the beer bottle coming from the direction Ms. Garlucci was standing. It's my determination she assaulted me and needs to be punished for it."

"This is all a big mistake," Mercedes insisted. "Sam Ivey, my boyfriend, can vouch for me."

"Who is Sam Ivey?"

"Must be a newbie," Elvira whispered under her breath.

The cop's head whipped around. "Did you call me a name?"

"I would never call an upstanding law enforcement official a derogatory name."

"I think you did. I was going to let you go, but I'm fed up with you running your mouth. A little time behind bars will give you time to think before you speak."

Elvira muttered something unintelligible under her breath and made some unhappy sounds.

Their trip to the police station was uneventful. The next hour passed by in a blur. The body search. The fingerprinting. The mugshot. During the booking process, Mercedes' purse and phone were confiscated.

She could hear Elvira down the hall whining and complaining, and she almost felt sorry for whoever was booking her.

Swapping out her clothes for a jail uniform was the last straw. Mercedes gritted her teeth, fighting back angry tears. Would she have a permanent record? Surely, striking an officer wasn't a felony—or was it? But then, she wasn't the person who hit him.

She thought about the time she and Autumn had been arrested after the death of a local news reporter. Being locked up was no picnic, but she didn't remember it smelling horrible.

What if the judge didn't believe her? What if he charged her with a crime she didn't commit? As far as Mercedes knew, she didn't have a record. Although she had been involved in a few questionable incidents, most recently involving the death of Sam's ex.

No matter how hard they tried, it seemed the Garlucci family was never far from criminal activity.

Mercedes went through the motions, walking alongside the guard to the end of the long hall, through the metal door, into another hall lined with jail cells.

It was all coming back to her. Elvira was right. It smelled bad. Like urine mingled with body odor. The guard opened the door on the right and motioned Mercedes into the holding cell.

She cast a furtive glance around the room. Old. Young. Bored. Agitated. Tired. The female occupants covered the spectrum of humanity. Most barely looked her way, all dealing with their own misery.

Mercedes found an empty bunk near the hall and perched on the edge.

A woman sporting cropped brown locks, in her late thirties, if she had to guess, sauntered over. She plopped down next to Mercedes, a little too close for comfort.

Mercedes moved away.

"What are you in for?"

"Assault. What about you?"

"Drug trafficking. You got any connections?"

"For what?"

"Drugs."

"Nope." Mercedes rested her elbows on her legs.

"Who did you assault? Your old man?"

"No."

"Not very chatty, are you?"

"This isn't my idea of a good time. So, yeah. Maybe I'm not feeling too talkative."

"You assault a kid? Cuz we don't take kindly to abusing kids around here," Cropped said.

"It was a cop."

"A cop?" Cropped burst out laughing. "Good luck with that one."

"I didn't do it."

"Yeah, and I'm Mother Teresa."

"Seriously. Anyway, I'm not in the mood for company."

"Suit yourself." Cropped slowly stood and walked away. She huddled with a couple of other women. They looked Mercedes way and started laughing.

She slumped on the bed, slid her hands behind her head, and closed her eyes. Two days in jail. Maybe not two, but if Elvira's statement was true, it would be a day and a half.

There was no sense in calling anyone. Dernice, Luigi, and Autumn would let Pete and Carlita know what had happened. Maybe Sam could pull some strings and get her out. Either way, it was shaping up to be a long night.

"Mercedes!"

Mercedes bolted upright at the familiar voice. It was Elvira. Elvira was nearby.

"Over here."

Swinging her legs over the side of the bunk, she peered into the adjacent cell.

Elvira stood in the corner, crooking her finger.

Mercedes trudged over. "Hey, Elvira."

"Did you make your allotted call?"

"No."

"Why not?"

"Because Dernice, Luigi, and Autumn will let everyone know what happened. If they can't get me out of here, there's no sense in bothering them this late at night."

"I called Dernice. She wanted to know if we'd seen Cool Bones. You see him?"

Mercedes shook her head. "No. Did you?"

"Nope. And I doubt we're going to. He's being held in another area. You're never gonna guess what they arrested him for."

Chapter 3

Mercedes grasped the jail cell bars and lowered her voice. "What did the cops arrest Cool Bones for?"

"You gotta guess."

"Drug trafficking?"

"Nope."

"Destroying private property? He and the Jazz Boys pulled a rockstar move and trashed a hotel suite while they were on the road."

"Nope, but that would have been a lot more fun."

"Hit and run."

"Not even close," Elvira said.

"I'm tired of guessing. Just tell me."

"Murder."

Mercedes' mind whirled. Cool Bones. Salt of the earth. Easygoing, laid back, gentle soul who was the best tenant, the best neighbor she could've ever asked for. "You're kidding."

"I wish I was. Dernice didn't have the details. After we got hauled away, they tracked down the Jazz Boys. Apparently, some woman claims she has proof that he murdered a bookie or runner years ago."

"Linked to illegal gambling?" Mercedes asked. "So, this was some sort of cold case murder?"

"From what the band members told Dernice, it happened a couple of decades ago." Elvira continued. "I guess the chick was able to get the attention of investigators. They dug up the guy's body and have some sort of evidence linking Cool Bones to the death."

Mercedes let out a low whistle. "I think it's a setup. No way did Cool Bones kill someone."

Elvira grimaced.

"You think he might have?"

"He's not as squeaky clean as he seems. Remember when I had the hots for him?"

"How can I forget? You were so hot for him, you painted his portrait."

"I like to check out potential mates, if you know what I mean. I did a background check on Cool Bones," Elvira said.

"And?"

She pointed her thumbs down. "He has a rap sheet."

"For what?"

"Petty theft, illegal gambling. There may have been something else, but I can't remember it off the top of my head."

"So the bookie thing might be legit," Mercedes said. "I mean, nobody is perfect."

"The cops must have something on him to arrest him after all this time."

"True." Mercedes mulled over Elvira's bombshell announcement. Was Cool Bones a killer? Decades of being on the lam was a long time. But why would the woman come forward now—after all these years? Perhaps the "witness" had an axe to grind.

"Fame isn't all it's cracked up to be," Elvira said. "Seems like it wasn't an issue until Cool Bones and his band became famous."

"Something isn't adding up."

"There's not much we can do to help him while we're in the slammer. If you're not going to make your allotted call, can I have it?"

"To call who?"

"Dernice. I need to remind her to check on Snitch. She's been doing better, but I think she's gonna be freaked out if I don't come home tonight."

Elvira had recently acquired a parrot for the sole purpose of having the bird spy on people, being her eyes and ears when she wasn't around. Snitch, although fulfilling her duty by tattling on everyone

23

and anyone, was high maintenance. Finnicky, moody, and demanding. In other words, Snitch kept Elvira hopping.

To everyone's surprise, the woman had become attached to the parrot and catered to her every whim. She'd even started taking Snitch with her to some of her security jobs.

"You can have my call," Mercedes said.

"Thanks." Elvira ran to the front and flagged the guard down. She briefly explained the situation.

Their initial answer was 'no', but Elvira continued nagging. After some back and forth, he and another guard, a woman, relented and escorted her out.

Mercedes returned to her cot and flopped down. She thought about poor Cool Bones. Being in jail for alleged assault was nothing compared to being charged with murder. Had her tenant taken someone's life? It seemed so out of character.

Maybe he'd been a different person back then. Bookies lived a stressful life. Losing money, dealing with shady individuals, struggling to stay off the authorities' radar. *If* Cool Bones had, in fact, been working as a bookie. So far, there was no confirmation of the fact.

Clank. Clank.

Mercedes rolled over, watching Elvira return to her cell. "Did you talk to Dernice?"

"Yeah. She's gonna keep an eye on Snitch. Thanks for letting me have your call."

"You're welcome."

"I told her to track Sam down to see if he can pull some strings and get us before the judge tomorrow. Snitch might be okay tonight, but I don't want her plucking her feathers out again."

"Ma told me Gunner keeps asking about Snitch."

"She's been yakking about him too. I'm not sure what all bird dating entails. It's something I need to work on. But I won't be doing anything stuck in this jail cell."

"The sooner we can get out of here, the better," Mercedes said.

"Cropped," who had apparently been eavesdropping, sauntered over. "You got someone who can spring us?"

"There is no us," Mercedes said. "I have a friend who might be able to get me and my neighbor out."

"Neighbor?" Cropped arched her eyebrow, eyeing Elvira with interest. "Did you assault someone too?"

"No. I was defending Mercedes. The cop didn't like me arguing her case and decided to lock me up for verbally resisting arrest."

Mercedes wrinkled her nose. "Is there such a thing? Verbally resisting arrest?"

"Who knows? Cops do whatever they want." Elvira leaned her head against the bars. "I had hoped to never see the inside of a jail cell again, but here we are. Although I must admit, it seems a little nicer than my previous incarceration at this location."

"When were you in jail?" Mercedes answered her own question. "Never mind. I remember now. It was the time you trespassed at Montgomery Hall."

"Let me tell you...I learned my lesson. I'll never try sneaking onto Tori Montgomery's property again. It was bad enough when her dog almost took my leg off, but that was nothing compared to her security guards tackling me, almost knocking me unconscious."

"You're lucky they didn't shoot you. It would have been justified."

"It was a dumb move. Trying to break into her place was a big mistake."

"What other time were you in jail?" Mercedes asked.

"Back a couple of years ago when I took the security job over at Darbylane Museum. *A Piece of Renaissance* artwork worth millions went missing. I made a stupid joke about swapping it out with one of my pieces. Next thing I know, everyone was pointing their fingers at me."

"You're right. I think Ma was questioned about the theft, if I remember correctly." Mercedes blew air through thinned lips. "I'm sorry you're here. I know you were only trying to help."

"At first, I was thinking poor Mercedes wouldn't survive in a jail cell and then I remembered." Elvira inspected her fingernails. "You've had the pleasure of three hots and a cot before."

"Not by choice," Mercedes sighed. "I have to say, this one takes the cake. I did not throw a beer bottle at that cop."

"You hit a cop with a beer bottle?" Cropped sneered. "They're gonna throw the book at you."

"I didn't do it."

"Yeah, and I didn't sell a few grams of cocaine to an undercover cop. It's a bum rap. I happened to be in the wrong place at the wrong time."

"Tell me about it." Mercedes pressed her fingers to her temples. She was developing a major migraine. "I think I'm going to get some rest."

Elvira tapped the metal bars. "Me too. I'm hoping we'll be out of this place by noon tomorrow."

Mercedes had her doubts. With a little luck, maybe Sam could pull a rabbit...or two...out of his hat and get both of them released. As far as Cool Bones was concerned, something told her he would need all the help he could get.

Chapter 4

"I don't know who to call first." Carlita darted from the living room to the kitchen. "Maybe Sam can help."

Pete pried his wife's cell phone from her hand, scrolled through the screen, and dialed Sam's cell phone number. The call went directly to voicemail. He left a brief message. "He's probably in bed. I don't recall seeing him at the Thirsty Crow."

"He stopped by early in the evening and had to leave," Carlita said. "What time is it?"

"After midnight. We might as well call it a day. Mercedes and Elvira won't be getting out at this hour."

"True." Carlita trudged after Pete while visions of Mercedes locked up and behind bars ran through her head. She was almost certain her daughter hadn't thrown the beer bottle. Mercedes had a temper but she would never strike another person, no matter how angry she may have been, unless it was self defense.

Elvira, on the other hand, was another story. She couldn't even begin to guess why the woman had been arrested, other than she must've driven the cops crazy, so they threw her in jail while they were at it.

And then there was Cool Bones. Dernice and Luigi claimed they spoke to the Jazz Boys and discovered he was being charged with a cold case murder. Something involving a bookie.

Dernice had done a little digging around and found out Carlita's tenant had a criminal record. Nothing exceptionally serious. Petty theft. Illegal gambling. The charges were old...a couple of decades old.

Reading between the lines, it appeared someone from Cool Bones' past spotted him being featured on the local news stations along with the Jazz Boys.

It had triggered a memory and now this person was convinced Cool Bones was a killer.

Although the details were fuzzy, Carlita believed the police had the wrong guy. She would bet her life Cool Bones wasn't a murderer.

"It'll be okay." Pete hugged her. "We'll get Mercedes out of jail ASAP and even Elvira if you want to."

"I'm more worried about Cool Bones."

"For good reason." Pete offered her a grim smile. "If what Dernice and Luigi said is true, he won't be going anywhere. The authorities must have some sort of concrete evidence to arrest him."

"They could have at least waited until the evening ended instead of making a scene and slapping the cuffs on him in front of friends and customers," Carlita said.

"Could be they knew he'd been traveling and found out he was back at the Thirsty Crow, their first opportunity to get him," Pete theorized.

"I suppose. Tomorrow is a new day." Carlita made quick work of getting ready for bed. She brushed her teeth and washed her face, peering at her reflection in the mirror. Some days she felt younger than her sixty plus years. While others, she felt older...much older. Tonight was one of them.

Pete waited for his wife to join him in bed, holding her close and assuring her it would all work out. He reminded her that Mercedes had been in jail before, which was true.

But something felt different this time. Maybe it was the circumstances. Maybe it was the fact the gung-ho cops had arrested two other people she cared deeply about. Yes, even Elvira.

A niggling voice in the back of her mind questioned whether Cool Bones could have committed murder. Under certain circumstances, people snapped and did things they later regretted. Had he taken another person's life? The police thought so. More than thought so. Clearly, they had some sort of proof.

She tossed and turned, worrying about her daughter and friends. Finally, early the next morning, Carlita crawled out of bed.

Rambo, who had been napping in the hall, trotted after her, stopping when he reached the front door.

"Some fresh air sounds good. Let's take a walk." Summer was in full swing, which meant she wouldn't need a jacket. Throwing on shorts and a lightweight shirt, Carlita jotted a quick note for Pete. She grabbed her cell phone and followed her pup down the stairs.

As if knowing where she wanted to go, Rambo led her home to Walton Square. With keys in hand, she let herself into Mercedes' apartment. Grayvie, the family's rescue cat, met her at the door.

"There's my Grayvie." After checking his food and water dish, Carlita did a perimeter search of the apartment, confirming her daughter hadn't somehow miraculously been released. The apartment was quiet and empty...too empty.

Stepping back into the hall, she lingered in front of Cool Bones' door. While Mercedes would be coming home soon, her tenant wouldn't be released until someone helped clear his name.

She hesitated, wondering if Sam was around. It was early…too early for a guided tour. It was also too early to bother him on a Sunday morning.

Mercedes had given Elvira her allotted call, which meant it was possible that Sam had no idea Mercedes was behind bars.

But Autumn, her other tenant, did. She was at the bar when Mercedes and Elvira were arrested. Which brought up another concerning thought. Cool Bones' arrest would be big news…news covered by all the local outlets.

Even if he was exonerated, the stigma of being arrested would linger long after. His years of sacrifice and hard work would be gone in a flash.

With renewed determination, Carlita exited the building and walked across the alley to Elvira's back door.

Suspecting Dernice was already awake, she rang the bell. Elvira's sister, with dark circles under her eyes, appeared moments later. "Hey, Carlita."

"Hello, Dernice. I hope I'm not bothering you."

"Not at all. I've been making phone calls this morning, trying to find someone who can get Mercedes and Elvira before a judge today."

"Any luck?"

"Nope." Dernice rubbed her forehead. "I worked my way down the list of every single person I could think of. Note to self—never get arrested on a weekend unless you don't mind being stuck behind bars."

"Sam might be able to help. I figured I would wait until he's up and around."

"Luigi and I talked to him last night. He's working on it, although he didn't sound hopeful. He's been out of the law enforcement loop for a while."

"Bummer." Carlita frowned. "They might have to sit tight for another night."

"Yep."

"Let me give it some thought." Carlita turned to go. "About Cool Bones. There's no chance of getting help for him."

"It's not looking good. I talked to Duke Drake, one of Cool Bones' friends who is part of his band. Apparently, a bookie was murdered here in Savannah years ago. Cool Bones knew the guy. He went to his apartment. They argued. Cool Bones claims the man was alive when he left."

"And then someone killed him?"

"Yep. It's only recently resurfaced. The cops have questioned Cool Bones about it. Something about a former neighbor, someone who lived in this guy's building, remembered seeing Cool Bones at his place the day he was murdered."

"Talk about being in the wrong place at the wrong time."

"So...the cops exhumed the body. He was a minor league baseball player who was into illegal betting. Anyway, he was buried with his favorite bat. They fingerprinted Cool Bones but couldn't get a match."

"And now, with advanced technology along with new information from the eyewitness, they decided to try again."

Dernice nodded. "Lo-and-behold, they matched Cool Bones' fingerprint to a set found on the bat he was buried with."

Carlita wrinkled her nose. "The guy wanted to be buried with the bat that killed him?"

"I'm sure stranger things have happened, but not this time. The bat he was buried with wasn't the murder weapon. At least, that's what I was told."

"It's amazing what technology can do these days. Still, I'm having a hard time believing it's true. I want to hear Cool Bones' side of the story."

"Like I said, Duke Drake, the band member who is up to speed with what's going on, confirmed he knew the deceased. Cool Bones even admitted to arguing with him but swears when he left the man's apartment, he was very much alive."

"There has to be more to the story," Carlita said.

"I'm a pretty good judge of character. Cool Bones might have a little history with the cops, but he's no killer."

Carlita thanked Dernice for trying to help. She and Rambo returned home and found Pete was up and waiting for them.

"I talked to Mark Fox a few minutes ago. I told him what happened and about Mercedes' arrest. He and Glenda know all the area judges. They're going to try to get Elvira and Mercedes both hearings this morning."

Carlita's heart skipped a beat. "That's wonderful news."

"They want to know if we can meet them down at the courthouse. The judge hears special cases starting at ten."

"Absolutely." While Carlita ran to the bathroom to freshen up, Pete let Mark know they would be there at ten on the dot.

With a few minutes to spare, Carlita grabbed their checkbook along with a credit card and they took off for the quick trip across town.

Mark and Glenda Fox were already waiting for them on the courthouse steps when they arrived.

"Thank you for offering to help." Carlita hugged her friends. "I'm sure Mercedes will be thrilled to get out."

"Elvira is also locked up," Pete reminded her.

"Yes. Elvira, as well."

"Elvira Cobb?" Glenda wrinkled her nose. "I'm inclined to let her sit and stew."

To say there was some bad blood between Glenda and Elvira was putting it mildly. Elvira, a former member of SAS, Savannah Architectural Society, of which Glenda was the president, had been a thorn in her side. Correction—in the entire committee's side, particularly after purchasing her historic building and promptly making unapproved changes to the structure.

"I'm sure you are. In her defense, she was trying to help Mercedes when she got arrested."

"So, she did something nice?" Glenda asked. "Color me shocked."

"Elvira is mellowing out in her old age," Pete said. "I suppose, in part because she spends all of her energies hunting for treasure and chipping away at my basement."

"How is the project going?" Mark asked. "Last I heard, it was moving slowly."

"At a snail's pace now that it's been designated an archaeological site. I let Elvira in once a week to sift through the loose dirt."

"Has she found anything?" Glenda asked.

"A few baubles and trinkets. Nothing earth-shattering. We're waiting for a special team to arrive to assess the progress. They specialize in designated excavation sites," Pete said.

"In the meantime, she's connected with an Alaska gold-mining company and is leaving in a few weeks to dig for gold."

"Alaska," Glenda said. "I think the final frontier is the perfect place for her."

"In the meantime, I feel like maybe we should try getting her released as well," Carlita said.

"Your call. I'm sure it will cost a few bucks to have them both released," Mark warned.

Pete patted his pocket. "I have my American Express Gold Card ready to go."

Passing through security, the foursome took the elevator to the second floor. While Carlita, Pete and Glenda waited in the hall, Mark, who had phoned ahead and spoke with the judge on duty, slipped inside for a brief consultation.

He returned moments later. "It's a go. The bailiffs are heading to the jail to pick up Elvira and Mercedes and bring them before the judge. If all goes well, they'll be out of here by noon."

"Thanks, Mark." Pete patted his arm. "We owe you one."

"No problem. I'm glad we could help."

Glenda glanced at her watch. "I hate to run, but we have a Sunday brunch meeting in City Market we can't miss."

"Thank you for helping." Carlita pressed her hand to her chest. "Stop by Ravello's anytime. Lunch is on me."

"Or at the Parrot House. In fact, give us a call, and Carlita and I will meet you for dinner."

"It's a deal." Glenda, with husband Mark by her side, stepped into the nearby elevator, waving goodbye right before the door closed.

Carlita waited until they were gone. "Let's head into the courtroom to wait."

Pete crossed his fingers. "Fingers crossed the judge shows leniency. Maybe we'll get lucky and he'll drop the charges."

Carlita grimaced. "We're talking about Elvira. The best we can hope for is she's smart enough to keep her mouth shut."

Chapter 5

Ping.

"Is someone texting you?" Pete leaned over his wife's shoulder.

"Sam. He had some suggestions on how to get Mercedes out of jail. I told him Mark and Glenda pulled a few strings. I also texted Tony to let him know what was going on. Sam is on his way."

"Here?"

"Yeah. I gave him the judge's name. He doesn't know the guy but wants to be here for moral support, a show of solidarity."

"Sam's a good guy."

"Very good. Mercedes likes...loves him. Although I'm not sure if she's in love with him anymore."

Ever since Natalie, his ex's death, Mercedes had struggled with trust issues. Toss in the taste of freedom, of having a place of her own, and Carlita suspected her daughter was enjoying her newfound independence.

As much as Carlita liked Sam, her daughter's happiness mattered most. And she was careful not to try to influence her. If Sam and Mercedes stuck it out and eventually married, she would be thrilled.

If Mercedes ended their relationship and moved on with her life, Carlita would fully support her decision. Mother and daughter had come a long way...a very long way since Vinnie Senior's death. Both had become independent, capable, and strong women, something she was extremely proud of.

As far as Carlita's relationship, Pete complemented her in so many ways. He loved his wife unconditionally, had accepted her and her family, even embracing their mafia ties with open arms.

Of course, Pete had skeletons in his own closet. Questionable ancestors, murky family history, which circled back around to the Parrot House and his pirate ancestry, a heritage which might—or might not—pay off in spades.

"He should be here any minute." Carlita tugged at her shirt, her armpits growing damp as the minutes ticked by and the judge began hearing special circumstance cases.

A movement near the door caught her attention. It was Sam. He slipped into the courtroom and made his way over. "How's it going?" he whispered.

"There's no sign of Mercedes or Elvira yet. Mark and Glenda got them a special hearing, or whatever you call it. They should be here anytime."

One right after another, prisoners appeared before the judge, some with straightforward cases while others were more complex. She wondered about Cool Bones and made a mental note to track down his band members to try to figure out how she could help.

The group seen by the judge exited through a door to the right. As soon as they were gone, a door on the other side of the room opened and the bailiff escorted a new group of inmates in.

Mercedes and Elvira were among the last. They were led to the seats just vacated. Following the same procedure, the inmates went before the judge, stating their case, admitting or denying their crime. Some were released while others were given specific instructions and sent back to jail pending another hearing.

Finally, it was Mercedes' turn. The bailiff led her to the podium. When prompted, she stated her full name.

He picked up a sheet of paper and studied it. "It says here you struck Officer Perkins in the back of the head with a beer bottle." He peered at her over the rim of his glasses. "Did you throw a beer bottle at him last night during an arrest?"

"No, your honor. I was in the vicinity, but I wasn't the person who threw the bottle," Mercedes said.

"Officer Perkins claims you were the only one who could have thrown it."

"There was a guy standing nearby. I didn't see him do it, but it could have been him."

"Do you know the man who was arrested last night at the nightclub?"

"Yes, your honor. He's my neighbor and a tenant in my building."

"So...you and he have a close relationship?"

"We're friends," Mercedes said.

"And you were upset he was being arrested," the judge pressed.

"I was. I mean, the cops could have waited until later instead of blowing into the bar with guns blazing and causing a scene."

"So, you think they should have waited outside until the evening ended instead of arresting your friend when they had the chance?"

"You asked for my opinion. I think they could have handled it better," Mercedes replied.

The judge cleared his throat. "I took the liberty of doing a little research. You've been arrested before."

"I have. I was also cleared of wrongdoing."

"But here you are again."

"Unfortunately."

The judge shuffled through his papers. "You were arrested along with Elvira Cobb, who is here in my courtroom. Where is she?"

The bailiff grasped Elvira's arm and led her to the front.

"Elvira Cobb...Elvira Cobb," the judge repeated. "Why does your name sound familiar?"

"I've been arrested a time or two. You look familiar. I believe you heard my case when I was wrongly accused of stealing artwork from the Darbylane Museum," Elvira said.

"Ah. I remember you now. You were acting foolishly, throwing out outlandish accusations. I almost held you in contempt of court," the judge said.

"Keep your mouth shut, Elvira," Carlita whispered under her breath.

"I may have spoken my mind," she admitted. "However, might I point out I was cleared of wrongdoing as well."

The judge removed his glasses, and began chewing on the end, thoughtfully studying Mercedes and Elvira. "Two women. Multiple arrests clogging up the court system with your antics."

"I wouldn't call them antics," Mercedes argued. "Again, your honor, I respectfully insist I did not throw a beer bottle at the officer."

Her voice rose an octave, clearly becoming aggravated with the accusation.

"Are you arguing with me, Ms. Garlucci?" he demanded.

"I'm stating my case. Isn't that why I'm here? To explain my side?"

"Oh no." Carlita rolled her eyes. This hearing was heading south...and fast. It was about as bad as it could get, but then...

Elvira stepped forward. "If I may, your honorary distinguishedness. Mercedes and I are victims of circumstances. Innocent bystanders, if you will, inadvertently caught in the crosshairs of criminal justice. We apologize for being here today. In fact, I would give anything to be somewhere else right now."

"I suppose you would." He slid his glasses on, drumming his fingers on the desk. "I think you two need to learn a lesson. One that will stick this time."

"A lesson?" Mercedes asked. "You mean like community service?"

The judge called the bailiff over. Talking in low voices, he motioned to the women. The bailiff chuckled and nodded.

He took his place off to the side, and the judge turned his attention back to the women. "I'm fining each of you five hundred dollars for disturbing the peace, impeding an arrest, and resisting arrest."

He continued. "I'll drop assaulting an officer. Officer Perkins didn't see you throw the bottle, and no eyewitness has come forward."

"Thank you." Mercedes clasped her hands. "Thank you, your honor."

"I'm not done. I'm mandating community service. Today is Sunday. On Tuesday of this week, I want both of you to report to the Savannah-Burnham Police Department for a full day of picking up trash."

Elvira made a choking sound. "Picking up trash on the streets?"

"On the streets, the sidewalks, in the squares. A full workday of trash pickup."

"This bites," Elvira muttered under her breath.

"What did you say?"

"Nothing."

"Because I'm tempted to send you right back to jail, Elvira Cobb."

"I would be pleased to pick up trash," Elvira said. "Thank you, your honor for such a fair and balanced punishment."

"Let me say I'm truly sorry Officer Perkins was struck. I hope the person who threw the bottle is caught," Mercedes said. "I would like to express my appreciation to you for fitting us in and hearing our side of the story this morning."

"You're dismissed."

The bailiff escorted Mercedes and Elvira out of the room.

Carlita gathered up her belongings. "Where to?"

"The bailiff will take them to the cashier's counter. We can meet them downstairs to pay the fine and get them out of here." Sam led the way out of the courtroom and held the door. "It could have been worse."

"I agree," Carlita said. "Paying a fine and performing community service seems like a fair compromise."

Pete pinched his thumb and index finger together. "Elvira was this close to being thrown back in jail."

"I think she realized it," Carlita said. "Thank goodness the judge dropped Mercedes' assault charge."

"Which is considered a serious offense," Pete said.

"She's lucky," Sam agreed. "However, something tells me when Mercedes and Elvira find out what their community service and picking up trash entails, they might not be as excited about their punishment."

"What does it entail?" Carlita asked.

"I would rather not spoil the surprise," Sam said. "As luck would have it, I have a morning tour on Tuesday, which means I'll be around when they hit the streets."

Chapter 6

"Cool Bones is in deep doo." Mercedes sifted through her purse, making sure she had her wallet and cell phone returned from the jail's clerk. "We need to try to figure out what happened."

"I'm already a step ahead of you," Carlita said. "While we were waiting, I contacted Duke Drake. He's been a Jazz Boy for years. I know he and Cool Bones are close. He's agreed to meet us at your place."

Moving at a brisk pace, the group trekked back to Walton Square and gathered inside Mercedes' apartment. Autumn, who must've been watching for them, showed up moments after they arrived.

 While they waited for Duke, Elvira and Mercedes filled her in on going before the judge and their sentence, picking up trash on Tuesday.

"I-I have a smidgen of bad news," Autumn said.

"About the arrest?" Sam prompted.

"Actually, it's about all three arrests."

"Great," Mercedes groaned. "I'm already thinking the community service sentence is bad enough."

"You're going to be on the six o'clock news," she blurted out.

"On the news?" Elvira stared at her. "You're running a segment about what happened last night? What kind of friend are you?"

"Not me. Another local news station. I caught wind of it and thought you might like to know."

"Hopefully, they won't mention Ravello's, the pawn shop or Pete's businesses," Mercedes said.

"Or my investigative and security services companies," Elvira added.

"I honestly don't know," Autumn said. "What I can tell you is I noticed a news van parked outside the pawn shop a couple of hours ago. I haven't had a chance to ask Tony if the reporters were in there snooping around."

"This is his first day back to work after his long family vacation." Carlita's middle son had taken his wife and daughter on an extended vacation, a road trip to New York, to show them around and spend time with his brother Paulie, wife Gina and the kids. It had been a well-deserved and long overdue break.

While they were gone, Carlita had been working on a special surprise for the growing family. Pulling it off was no small feat, but Bob Lowman, her construction manager, had come through, persuading his guys to put in a little overtime to ensure the project's timely completion. Throwing some extra cash and bonuses their way had also helped.

"I'll go see if Tony has a sec to chat," Mercedes said.

Carlita held a finger to her lips. "Not a peep about the family surprise."

Mercedes made a zipping motion across her lips. "Mum's the word." She hurried out of the apartment, returning a short time later with her brother trailing behind.

"Mercedes doesn't look any worse for the wear." Tony nudged Elvira's foot with his shoe. "You're looking a little rough."

"A little rough?" Elvira scowled. "Maybe you should spend the night with a bunch of yapping women in a cramped jail cell and we'll see who looks worse for the wear."

"I'm messing with you." Tony patted her arm. "Ma told me how you came to Mercedes' defense last night and ended up getting arrested."

"It was an unfortunate incident. Mercedes and Elvira paid the fine. They'll do a little community service on Tuesday and we can put the entire episode behind us. I'm afraid Cool Bones won't be so lucky." Carlita filled her son in on what they knew so far. "Duke Drake, Cool Bones' close friend and band member will be by soon to hopefully help us figure out our next step."

Tony let out a loud whistle. "Cool Bones and his band finally get their lucky break, receiving a prestigious award to boot, and now this."

"The cops must have a strong case or some sort of evidence to arrest him," Carlita said. "Dernice mentioned something about a fingerprint on the deceased's bat."

Mercedes made a choking sound. "The guy was killed with his own bat?"

"No. He was a minor league baseball player who supposedly requested he be buried with his special bat."

"So they exhumed the body and matched a fingerprint to Cool Bones?" Tony asked.

"In a nutshell. An eyewitness identified Cool Bones as being with the guy shortly before his death," Carlita summarized. "Unless we can prove otherwise, I'm afraid he might end up being convicted of murder."

"I told Mercedes and Elvira they're probably going to be on television," Autumn said. "I noticed a competitor's news van parked out in front of the pawn shop earlier. I'm guessing they were there trying to get a scoop."

"Sure were. I didn't give them any ammo. The reporter wasn't taking no for an answer. I wouldn't be surprised if he eventually dug something up."

"You didn't mention my name, did you?" Elvira asked.

"He and his news crew already had your name. I'm pretty sure they were heading over to your office when they left the pawn shop."

"Dernice better not have told them anything. I'm going to call her right now." Elvira dialed her sister's number.

"Hey, Elvira. Is Carlita getting ready to spring you?"

"We're already out. I'm at Mercedes' place."

"The judge let you go?"

"Yes. We paid a fine, and he saddled us with community service. By the way, I have you on speaker."

"Hey, all. What kind of community service?"

"Picking up trash on Tuesday. All day in downtown Savannah."

Dernice burst out laughing. "This I gotta see."

"Yeah. Yeah. Whatever. I'm calling because a local news reporter was sniffing around earlier today, trying to get the scoop on what happened last night," Elvira said. "Did he come by the office?"

"He did. I think his name was Johnson something," Dernice said.

"Johnson is a snake," Autumn said.

"I hope you showed him the door."

"You bet. He didn't get anything out of me."

"He can go pound sand. He better not make up a bunch of lies. I'll sue him for slander."

"You didn't let me finish. I didn't say anything. However, someone else did."

"Who was it?" Elvira demanded. "I'll fire them."

"I think you should watch the report and see for yourself."

Elvira thanked her sister and ended the call. "My day just keeps getting better and better."

"At least we're out of jail," Mercedes said. "I would rather have a bad day at home than a bad day behind bars."

Autumn cleared her throat. "You won't have to wait until this evening. Channel 2 runs a Sunday special news report. It airs every thirty minutes."

"Oh goodie. I can hardly wait," Elvira said sarcastically.

Ding. Ding. The doorbell rang. Carlita ran to the window. "It's Duke. I'll go let him in."

63

She hustled downstairs to greet the Jazz Boys' bandmember. "Thank you for coming by so quickly. Have you heard from Cool Bones?"

"Yeah. He's bummed out."

"I'm sorry to hear that." She ushered him up the stairs and into Mercedes' apartment. "I believe you know everyone here."

"I do."

"We want to help clear Cool Bones of the charges," Carlita said. "Tell us everything you know."

"There's not much to tell. The guy's name was Rudy McCoy. He was a minor league baseball player and a bookie. Way back when, Cool Bones was also a bookie, trying to make a buck while trying to get the band going."

"For how long?"

"A short time. At least, that's what he told me. He was more of an outsider, never in the clique of the bookie group," Duke said.

"How did he meet Rudy McCoy?"

"The two worked the same territory over on the outskirts of town. From what Cool Bones remembers, this Rudy guy was talking smack, spreading lies about him and also stealing an important customer. Cool Bones found out where he lived. He confronted him at his apartment. They argued. Cool Bones left his place. End of story."

"And they never crossed paths again?" Tony asked. "I mean, if they were in the same line of work, they would have run into each other again."

"Cool Bones was on his way out. He was getting out of the bookie business," Duke explained. "Like I said, the guy was a baseball player. They did a bunch of fingerprinting at the scene but could never match it to anyone."

Duke continued. "Cool Bones was initially a suspect, but there was no proof. Mrs. Culpepper, the dead guy's landlord, recognized him after seeing us being presented with the Georgia Jazz Music Award. She phoned the investigator,

65

insisting she saw him with McCoy shortly before his death. The rest is history."

"Ah." Carlita tapped her foot on the floor. "Thinking they had sufficient reason; the investigators exhumed the body, examined the bat, his favorite bat, and found a print matching Cool Bones' print."

"Does Cool Bones have any idea how his print got on the bat?"

"The guy threatened him with it. Cool Bones grabbed it to stop him. He left right after," Duke said. "Like I said, they fingerprinted him at the time it happened, but couldn't confirm. I guess with new technology, they tried again and were able to get a match."

"Perhaps it was another bookie he ticked off." Carlita paced. "Maybe it was the landlord, the person who reported Cool Bones."

"From what Cool Bones told me, she's old. Even back then, I doubt she murdered a baseball player, a man younger and stronger than she was." Duke told them he planned to visit his friend. "He's pretty down right now."

"I'm hoping to go see him tomorrow," Carlita said. "We want to help."

"Cool Bones always brags about the Garlucci family's uncanny ability to solve crimes."

"Does he ever mention me?" Elvira asked. "Cuz I'm pretty good at crime solving myself."

"He showed me the portrait you sketched of him. He said..." Duke's voice drifted off.

"What did he say?" Elvira prompted.

"It was nothing. Nothing significant."

"I bet he was telling you he once had a thing for me."

"No." Duke thought about it. "I don't believe he ever mentioned being attracted to you."

"It doesn't matter." Elvira flung her arm around Carlita's shoulder. "We're a close-knit neighborhood and family. If one of us is in trouble, the others will do whatever it takes to help."

"He's gonna need it." Duke told them he'd already called the jail, inquiring about visiting hours. "I made an appointment to see him at nine, the first time slot open for visitors."

"I have a couple of errands to run," Carlita said. "When you see him, tell him I'll be there around eleven."

"They only allow two visits and two visitors per visit per day," Duke said.

"I'm kinda tied up in the morning," Elvira said. "If you wait until later in the afternoon, I'll go with you."

"Or me," Pete offered.

"I want to go with Ma," Mercedes said. "Something tells me we need to kick this investigation into high gear ASAP."

Chapter 7

As soon as Duke left, Carlita hopped on the internet and snagged a time slot for her and Mercedes to visit their tenant and began researching Rudy McCoy's death. Several old news stories popped up, all of them corroborating what Duke had said.

The minor league baseball player, a known bookie, had been murdered. Although no murder weapon had ever been found, it was determined he'd died from blunt force trauma.

"Having any luck, Ma?" Mercedes carried a chair over to the computer desk.

"Some." She shared what she'd found. "I was wondering why the authorities would allow McCoy's bat to be buried with him, considering it may have been a potential murder weapon."

"Unless they tested it and ruled it out," Pete said. "I wonder if a fingerprint is the only incriminating evidence they found against Cool Bones."

"Circumstantial evidence. Witness statement. Being able to place Cool Bones at the man's apartment around the time of the murder," Carlita theorized. "Who knows? Only a jury can decide if there's ample evidence to convict him."

"It's not a slam dunk," Elvira said. "Although stacking up the evidence could help sway a jury. The argument. The eyewitness. The fingerprints. He's gonna need a good attorney to get him out of this one."

"Unless we can figure out who the killer is," Carlita said.

"It's almost showtime." Mercedes turned the television on. Tony, Pete, Carlita, Autumn, Sam and Elvira gathered in the living room. She flipped through the channels until reaching Channel 2 news.

The outer bell rang. "I bet it's Dernice." Elvira took off. She reappeared seconds later with her sister close behind. "The news is on. I figured you would be watching it."

"They're reporting on the weather," Mercedes said. "Hopefully, it will be a small clip at the end, right after the local sports, and no one will be watching."

"I called everyone I could think of and told them to tune in."

Elvira punched her sister in the arm. "Why did you do that?"

"Because this is your moment of fame. Soak it up. Enjoy."

"I was arrested and thrown in jail," Elvira gritted out. "Who needs that kind of fame?"

"I thought it was pretty cool."

"Pretty cool? I wish it had been you."

"Here we go." Carlita held a finger to her lips. "Breaking news from downtown Savannah."

She turned the volume up. The room's occupants grew quiet. Johnson, the reporter, stood in front of the Thirsty Crow. He interviewed the bar's owner, interviewed a couple who were on hand the previous night, describing it as a chaotic scene with patrons booing the cops when Cool Bones was arrested.

A photo of Carlita's tenant flashed across the screen. Johnson explained why he'd been arrested and then an old photo of the original crime scene, along with a black and white snapshot of the victim, appeared.

"A new cold case task force has been assembled. Authorities are hopeful this murder case, along with several others, will be solved by year's end."

Johnson switched the microphone to his other hand. "Not only did Charles Benson, who goes by the stage name Cool Bones, have many supporters inside the bar, Mercedes Garlucci, a Savannah local, was arrested after striking an officer with a beer bottle. During the melee Elvira Cobb, owner of

EC Investigative Services and EC Security Services attempted to interject herself in the situation and was arrested as well."

Clips of Mercedes and Elvira being escorted to the cop car appeared on the screen.

Mercedes pressed her hands to her cheeks. "I look awful."

"I think you look cute." Sam hugged her.

"I guess I don't look too bad," Elvira said. "Maybe a smidgen ticked. It's better than looking like a doofus."

"You look ticked," Carlita agreed.

"Because Officer Perkins was being a real jerk," Elvira said. "And a bully."

Dernice rubbed her palms together. "Johnson is getting to the good part. I hope he didn't cut it out."

Her sister eyed her suspiciously. "Good part?"

"Before I was able to escort him and his news crew out of the office."

Johnson reappeared, now standing near Elvira's office door. "While doing some digging around, I found Ms. Cobb's arrest wasn't her first run-in with the law." He told viewers about her two previous arrests. "We weren't able to get any of her employees to talk, but we found an interesting source of information."

The camera jiggled and panned at a rapid rate. Snitch sat on her perch, warily eyeing the strangers.

"Hello."

"Hello," Snitch replied.

Dernice, who was off screen, introduced the bird. "This is Snitch."

"Hello, Snitch." Johnson stepped closer to the birdcage. "Do you know Elvira Cobb?"

"Annoying Elvira," Snitch squawked. "Cheapskate. Cheapskate."

"What?" Elvira sprang to her feet. She lunged forward, getting right in her sister's face. "Who taught Snitch to say that?"

"She must've overheard some employees talking," Dernice said. "When I realized Snitch might not paint you in the most flattering light, I hustled Johnson and his cameraman out of the building."

"Lock her up. Lock her up."

Off camera, echoes of laughter could be heard.

A smiling Johnson reappeared on the sidewalk. "There you have it, folks. Snitch appears to be a disgruntled EC Security Services employee. As far as the investigation is concerned, details are still unfolding. Tune in to the six o'clock report for updates."

"Snitch isn't disgruntled. I'm going to find out who taught her to say that and make them eat their words," Elvira ranted. "How disrespectful and to be caught on camera to boot."

"She seems to have a bountiful vocabulary," Pete said.

"Which is one of the reasons I wanted her. She has a mind like a steel trap. Anything you say…"

"Can and will be used against you," Mercedes quipped.

"Adopting the bird is backfiring big time." Carlita clamped a hand over her mouth, trying not to laugh. "Maybe it will drum up some business. Free publicity and all."

"Drum up business?" she roared. "My loyal and faithful companion called me a cheapskate and annoying."

"And to lock you up," Tony snickered. "I thought it added a little levity to the situation."

Elvira grabbed her bag off the couch and marched toward the door, a thunderous expression on her face. "Snitch and I are going to have a nice long chat."

She stormed out of the apartment, still muttering and mumbling under her breath. The alley door slammed so hard it shook the wall.

Mercedes darted to the window, watching her neighbor march across the alley and disappear inside her apartment.

Dernice started to follow behind.

Carlita stopped her. "You might want to give her a few minutes to cool off."

"Elvira's just blowing off steam. She loves Snitch. I'm sure she's feeling a little betrayed." Dernice tapped Mercedes' arm. "What time is your community service on Tuesday?"

"We have to report to the Savannah-Burnham Police Department at eight a.m."

"Are you gonna be done in time for Shelby's baby shower?"

"I'm not hosting it until seven, so we should be safe, unless they make us stay overtime," Mercedes said.

"I don't want to postpone it. She's going to have the baby any day now."

"Shelby looks like she's ready to pop. It's a good thing Tony and the family made it home before she went into labor. I'll be here for the party." Whistling under her breath, Dernice exited the apartment. The alley door closed, much quieter than what Elvira had done.

Mercedes slumped down on the couch and leaned her head back. "A nice bubbly bath and a good night's rest sounds wonderful."

"I bet it does," Carlita said. "I'm sure Cool Bones would be thrilled to be home."

"With Carlita Garlucci-Taylor on the case, he has a shot at getting his name cleared," Pete said.

"If I was being accused of murder, I would want you on my team," Autumn chimed in.

"Based on what we've learned so far, he'll need all the help he can get," Sam said.

"At the risk of stating the obvious, bookies often have mafia ties," Tony said. "You sure you wanna start digging around?"

"I'm not thrilled with the idea," Carlita admitted. "If we don't help Cool Bones, who will?"

"His daughter Jordan lives in Atlanta. I wonder if he plans on telling her what's going on," Mercedes said.

"It will be up to him. Hopefully, he'll be exonerated before she finds out," Carlita said. "If we have a shot at clearing his name, we're going to need his help."

"Cool Bones is my friend too," Sam said. "I can put out a few feelers down at the police station to get an idea of where the case stands."

"Any information will help," Carlita said. "Hopefully by this time tomorrow, we'll be hot on the trail of Rudy McCoy's cold case killer."

Chapter 8

Pete crossed his arms, casually leaning against the kitchen counter. "What are you doing, dear?"

"I have some energy to burn and figured now was the perfect time to work on my southern-style biscuits and gravy recipe with a pinch of Italian thrown in," Carlita said. "I think I mentioned surveying restaurant customers. Of course, they love our Italian dishes, but every once in a while, someone asks if we offer anything with a southern flair."

"I love biscuits and gravy." Pete leaned over her shoulder, playfully nuzzling her neck. "You smell good."

Carlita lifted her arm and sniffed her shirt. "I smell like bacon."

"I happen to love bacon." Pete placed a light kiss on her forehead and reached for an apron. "I want to help. Put me to work."

"The biscuits are in the oven and should be almost done."

The timer chimed. Pete slid a mitt on, opened the oven door and removed the baking sheet. "These look delicious. You made them from scratch?"

"From scratch, using simple ingredients. Flour, butter, milk, and even a pinch of baking soda." Carlita hustled over to the stove. "The bacon crisped up nicely. It's time to work on the gravy."

After heating the bacon grease, she stirred flour into the drippings, sprinkled salt and pepper, and added the milk, stirring constantly. As soon as it thickened, she added the crumbled bacon, chopped scallion and her secret ingredient—rosemary.

"I could eat this for dinner," Pete said.

"I was thinking about grilling pork chops."

"Why bother? This is a meal itself and will suit me fine."

"Dinner it is." Carlita grabbed plates from the cupboard. She placed warm biscuits on each plate and ladled a generous amount of gravy over the top. "I hope this tastes as good as it looks."

"I'm sure it will." Pete opened the fridge and rummaged around. "How about a side of fresh cut fruit?"

"You read my mind." Carlita carried the plates out onto the balcony. Pete wasn't far behind, juggling the bowl of fruit and bottles of sparkling water.

"I can't wait to dig in." He picked up his fork and cut off a chunk of thick, buttery biscuit. He rolled it around in the gravy and took a big bite. "This is delicious."

"You're not just saying that?"

"Nope."

Carlita cut through her biscuit. She dipped it in the gravy and nibbled the edge. "It is yummy. I'm not sure I would change a thing."

Rambo, who had been closely monitoring the meal, nudged Carlita's leg, looking for a treat. "I didn't forget about you." She reached into her apron pocket, grabbed a handful of his favorite dog treats and fed them to him. "I would let you try the gravy, but last time I mentioned table food to the vet, she said it was a no-no."

Content with his treats, the pup trotted over to his doggie bed and settled in.

While they ate, the couple discussed Cool Bones and his arrest. The more Carlita thought about it, the more convinced she was the authorities had arrested the wrong person. If true, they had matched a print to Cool Bones, but it wasn't from the murder weapon. As far as they knew, it was still missing.

A small niggling in the back of her mind reminded her of Cool Bones' rap sheet, although it was for minor crimes. Petty theft, illegal gambling which more than likely tied into the bookie business angle. People made mistakes. All things considered, his appeared to be more of a case of him being in the wrong place at the wrong time.

She didn't doubt Mrs. Culpepper had seen the victim and Cool Bones argue, but someone else must have been in the vicinity...someone the neighbor hadn't noticed.

And that someone was the person Carlita needed to figure out. Taking another bite, she mentally ticked off the list of things she wanted to ask him.

Pete waved his hand in front of his wife's face. "Earth to Carlita."

"Sorry. I was thinking about Cool Bones and the baby shower."

"Hopefully, Mercedes will make it home in time," Pete said. "As far as Cool Bones is concerned, your biggest hurdle will be communicating."

"Which is why I need to have all of my ducks in a row when Mercedes and I visit him."

"Are you sure you don't want me to go with you?"

"I appreciate the offer." Carlita squeezed his hand. "Mercedes seems to want to be involved, so if you're okay with it, I'll take her."

"She's already involved." Pete polished off his biscuit. "I wonder how Elvira and her bird are getting along."

Carlita grinned. "Did you see the look on her face when Snitch started talking?"

"It appears her plan of having her parrot spy on her employees has backfired. She seems attached to Snitch."

"I never pegged Elvira for an animal lover, but I have to say she is now."

"An animal lover who has met her match."

"She certainly has." Carlita slid her chair back and reached for Pete's empty plate. "It looks like someone is ready for seconds. I'll grab you another serving of food and a pen and paper to jot down some notes to ask Cool Bones when I get there tomorrow morning."

*****

At precisely eleven the next morning, Mercedes and Carlita checked in at the Savannah-Burnham Police Department's inmate visitor's desk. The clerk verified their appointment and reminded them they had thirty minutes from the moment they stepped into the corridor leading to the visitation rooms.

After collecting their personal belongings, to be held until the visit ended, and passing through the metal detector, mother and daughter followed a guard down the hall. Making a sharp left, they entered another, narrower hall.

Passing through a metal door, the guard waited until they were on the other side. The door closed behind them, clanking loudly.

Mercedes jumped, clutching her chest. "I hate that sound."

"I bet you do. You know who probably hates it even more?"

"Cool Bones. I wonder how he's holding up."

"We'll soon find out."

They entered a room off to the right. Cool Bones was already there, his head down and a look of utter defeat etched on his face.

The room's layout reminded Carlita of a voting booth with dividers on both sides. A stool. A small desk. Attached to the wall was a phone. Thick Plexiglas panels allowed visitors and inmates to see each other.

"You'll be at station ten."

"I see our...friend." Carlita, with Mercedes by her side, took her seat across from him. She lifted the telephone receiver and pressed the speaker button so her daughter could hear. "Hey, Cool Bones."

"Hello, Carlita, Mercedes."

"How are you holding up?"

He tipped his hand back and forth. "About as good as can be expected, I suppose."

"We're here to let you know we're going to figure out a way to help you. Tell us everything you know about Rudy McCoy."

Cool Bones' shoulders drooped. "Don't waste your time. The investigators think they have a slam dunk. It's no use."

"It's not a slam dunk case," Mercedes said. "You didn't kill the guy. Someone did and we're going to find out who it was."

Carlita opened the notepad she was allowed to bring with her and began jotting down notes. "Our first step is to check out the place where you and Mr. McCoy argued. Do you remember the address?"

"It's etched in my mind. The address is 2012 Gleason Street."

Mercedes repeated it. "Gleason Street doesn't ring a bell."

"It's not the best area of town," Cool Bones said. "I remember Mrs. Culpepper, the building owner and landlady. She was a snoopy woman. Rudy couldn't stand her. It's driving me nuts, how she's decided to come forward now, after all these years."

"That's an excellent question." Carlita tapped her pen on top of the notepad. "I know it was a long time ago, but it would be helpful if you could tell Mercedes and me exactly what happened."

"It won't be hard," he said. "I remember it like it was yesterday."

Chapter 9

Savannah, Georgia: 25 years ago.

"I gotta get this run done." Cool Bones sauntered down Gleason Street. Tilting his fedora at an angle, he strolled past the brick apartment buildings. It wasn't the best area of town, but it wasn't the worst either.

One could say Gleason Street was on the fringes. Single story homes with single car garages clustered together...until you crossed over to the 2000 block. The tidy homes were fewer and farther between, replaced by rectangular brick apartments.

Cool Bones had one more transaction to handle before he was officially out of the bookie business. He'd been jumped too many times. Robbed at knifepoint, his life threatened in back alleys and abandoned buildings. It wasn't worth it for the measly amount of money he was making.

Besides, he and his band, the Jazz Boys, were finally getting some gigs. And not just bars throwing a few bucks and a few beers their way on the weekends. They were signing on for honest-to-goodness paid performances.

This weekend was his last bookie run. As luck would have it, there was a little spot of trouble he needed to handle first. Rudy McCoy. Minor league baseball player, an up-and-coming bookie who was trying to muscle in on Cool Bones' best better. He needed this last "vig" or vigorish to put gas in the van and pay for the hotel for him and the band members.

Rudy was causing problems. Major problems, threatening to swoop in and steal the "vig." Cool Bones needed to make sure it didn't happen. He knew Rudy's routine. He was home, working on his next bet, working on his next cut.

He jogged left, reaching the three-story brownstone apartment. With a quick glance around, Cool Bones rang the bell.

"Who is it?" Rudy's rude snarl echoed through the cheap metal speaker.

"It's CB. Cool Bones."

"What do you want?"

"To chat?"

"About what?"

"Business."

"You got a deal for me?" Rudy asked.

"I have a business proposition," Cool Bones replied.

"C'mon up." Rudy buzzed him in.

Cool Bones entered the dark hallway.

Bang. A door at the end of the hall echoed.

Mrs. Culpepper, the landlady and building owner who kept a close eye on anyone who came by the building, appeared. Of course, Rudy couldn't stand her. He constantly complained she was always up in his business.

But then, who could blame the woman? A bookie was a less than reputable career choice. No doubt, McCoy had all kinds of unsavory characters showing up day and night.

Cool Bones climbed the stairs. Rudy's door flew open. He motioned his visitor inside. "Hurry up before Culpepper sees you."

"She already knows I'm here."

"The nosy bat is spying on me. Her eyesight is crap and yet she always seems to be around," Rudy griped.

"I'm sure she has her reasons," CB said.

"You got a new contact for me?"

"No." CB's eyes started to burn. "What's that smell?"

"I think I got a gas leak. The nosy witch refuses to do anything about it."

"Can we step outside and chat?"

Rudy grumbled under his breath. He grabbed his baseball bat, reluctantly following Cool Bones out of the hall, down the stairs and into the backyard.

"What's up with the bat?" Cool Bones gave him a side eye.

"Been getting some threats recently. I don't leave the apartment without it."

"Threats?"

"I think I might've stepped on a toe or two. Bookies are a paranoid bunch." Rudy leaned on the bat and changed the subject. "What do you have?"

"Stepped on whose toes?"

"Cray. You ever met him?"

"No, and I don't plan on it." Cool Bones shifted his feet. "Look. I'm getting out of the bookie business. My band and I have a sweet deal set up. I need this last vig to pay for gas and the hotel. My client said you offered him a better cut."

"Who was it?"

"Kent."

"Yeah. Kent's a good guy. You're charging him too much," Rudy said. "Business is business."

"I need this vig." Cool Bones, fists clenched, took a menacing step toward him.

"So do I." Rudy nervously licked his lips, tightening his grip on the bat. "You're the one who has been threatening me. I knew it."

"It wasn't me, but you're going to need to back down and stop contacting my customer."

"He's not your customer. Kent can work with whoever he wants."

Cool Bones could feel his blood pressure spike. "Not this time. I already told you. I need the cash."

Without warning, Rudy swung the bat at Cool Bones.

Anticipating the move, he easily sidestepped the man, grabbed hold of the bat, and wrestled it from him. "You're crazy, dude. I thought you were my friend."

"Bookies don't have friends," Rudy said breathlessly. "Let go of my bat."

Cool Bones, a good foot taller than McCoy, shoved the bat, knocking him to the ground. Disgusted, he tossed it next to him. "Man, I'm finished with you and this bettin' business."

He stalked off, furious at himself for letting McCoy get under his skin.

"You better never come back here!" Rudy yelled after him. "You'll be sorry. You hear me?"

*****

Cool Bones switched the telephone receiver to his other ear. "It was the last time I saw Rudy McCoy alive," he said.

Carlita crossed her arms. "Mrs. Culpepper must've seen Rudy swing at you when you were arguing in the backyard."

"You said Rudy mentioned a name. Cray," Mercedes prompted. "Did you ever find out who he was?"

"Nope. I told the cops during the initial investigation *and* when they picked me up last night. I don't think they believe me." Cool Bones rubbed his forehead. "I even offered to let the investigators have my old bookie journal. They weren't interested in it back then and they're not interested now because they already believe they have the killer—me."

Carlita blinked rapidly. "You kept a copy of the bets?"

"Yes, ma'am. I'm not sure why. I wish I could get my hands on it. It might jog my memory."

"What if Mercedes and I brought it to you?" Carlita snapped her fingers. "Let me ask the guard a quick question." She ran over to the door, had a word with the guard on duty, and returned. "You're allowed paper products, which means you can have it while you're in here."

Cool Bones' eyes lit. "Would you? Duke would go get it for me, but I hate to bother him."

"Absolutely."

"This will work out even better, since you have a key to my apartment."

"Why don't we plan on dropping it off at the front desk? Once you've had a chance to take a look at it, we can come back and figure out if there's anything worth following up on."

With a plan in place and Cool Bones in much better spirits, mother and daughter headed home to get ready to cover their shifts at Ravello's.

Pete was long gone. He and Gunner were at the Flying Gunner, repairing some minor damage from a recent group outing on board the pirate ship.

Carlita swapped out her summer clothes for her work uniform and headed back to Walton Square. She arrived to find Mercedes was already there, waiting tables.

With a quick stop in the kitchen, Carlita took her place at the hostess stand. The hours flew by. Tables filled. Hungry patrons arrived. Happy diners departed. All the while, she thought about Cool Bones being locked up and how discouraged he'd been.

Paisley, Steve Winters' girlfriend and new restaurant employee, arrived. Not only a new employee, but one of Ravello's best. Customers loved her. Employees loved her. To sum it up, she fit right in.

In fact, she and Mercedes were becoming close friends. Steve and Paisley, who had gotten behind on their bills at the tattoo shop, were working hard to dig out of their financial hole. Paisley often volunteered to cover extra shifts to help chip away at their debt.

Finally, Carlita's shift ended. She hung around to work on her purchase order.

Mercedes breezed into the kitchen. "I was hoping you hadn't left yet."

99

"I was trying to catch up on the books. We got slammed for a Monday."

"It felt like a Friday." Mercedes untied her apron and hung it on the hook. "Paisley offered to cover for me tomorrow."

"I almost forgot about your dash for trash." Carlita turned the computer off and reached for her purse. "I have the final list of dishes and games for the baby shower. Can you take a quick look at it to make sure I haven't missed anything?"

"Sure." Mercedes perused the list. "Looks good. I have the decorations ready to go. As long as I'm done with my community service by five, I should be all set."

"I was thinking I could come by around six to start decorating."

"Sounds good. If I'm not home, let yourself in." Mercedes handed the list back to her mother. "Did you want to swing by Cool Bones' place to look for the bookie journal?"

"That's an excellent idea." Reaching the apartment, Carlita waited in the hall for Mercedes to drop her things off at home. Using her main key, she let them into the apartment.

Cool Bones' saxophone sat in the corner, waiting to be picked up and played. The apartment was quiet...too quiet.

"I'm gonna check his plants to make sure they don't need water." Mercedes watered the plants while Carlita began searching the hall closet, the place where Cool Bones thought the journal might be located.

Starting at the top, she dug through the bins filled with music notes, photo albums, odds and ends accumulated over the years.

Near the bottom, Carlita found what she was looking for—the black bookie journal. "I found it."

She carried it to the kitchen counter and began flipping through the pages. "I forgot to ask Cool Bones for the date he and Rudy argued."

"I can find out." Mercedes slid her cell phone from her back pocket and searched for Rudy McCoy. "He was murdered on October 10, 2000."

"Thanks." Carlita rifled through the pages, stopping when she reached early October. She slipped her reading glasses on and worked her way down the page of entries. "Cool Bones' meeting with Rudy was one of his very last entries."

Mercedes leaned over her shoulder. "I have to say, he kept meticulous records. Maybe he'll see something we're missing."

Carlita snapped photos of the pages during the date in question. She started to close the book when something caught her eye.

"Hang on." She tapped the page. "Check it out. Do you see what I see?"

Chapter 10

"Cray. Right here in Cool Bones' handwriting is the name Cray," Mercedes said. "Maybe he forgot."

"It's entirely possible." Carlita studied the cryptic notes, written in code, a code only her tenant would understand. "There are a lot of names and numbers in here. This thing is twenty plus years old. I'm not sure I would remember names either."

Mother and daughter flipped through a few more pages before giving up on deciphering what it all meant.

"Hopefully it will come back to him." Carlita slowly stood. "I can't remember the last time I've been inside this apartment."

"Cool Bones is tidy." Mercedes swiped her finger across the counter. "Not a speck of dust."

"Unlike someone I know," Carlita teased.

"Hey, I try. I'm a busy woman. Besides, housework isn't at the top of my to-do list."

"You can keep the apartment any way you want. It's all yours." On the way out, Carlita shut the lights off and followed Mercedes into the hall. "I haven't asked in a while, but how is the single life suiting you?"

"It's awesome. I can write late at night and don't have to worry about bothering you. If I want to sleep in, I don't feel guilty. Knowing Sam is across the hall and Luigi is at the bottom of the stairs makes me feel safe."

"Nothing is going to get past an ex-cop and an ex-mob man."

"Nothing. Autumn and I...and Cool Bones have it made."

"We have a great group of tenants and I plan on keeping it that way." Heading back downstairs, Carlita swung by the pawn shop to check on Tony and fill him in on what they'd discovered. "I think this Cray person is the key. If we can figure out who Cray is, we're a step closer to proving Cool Bones didn't kill Rudy McCoy."

"It looks like you have your work cut out for you," Tony said. "Speaking of work cut out, I was thinking about Mercedes and Elvira and their community service."

"What about it?"

"I was talkin' to an employee who has done community service and trash time. It might not be their cup of tea," Tony said.

"I would think picking up trash for a day would be a piece of cake." Carlita snapped her fingers. "Knock it out and get it done."

"We'll see. I'll be curious to hear how they do."

Carlita turned to go and abruptly stopped. "How is Shelby?"

"Still having mild contractions. She's trying all the old tricks to induce labor. Spicy foods, lots of walking, you name it. Every day she's trying something new."

"I know it's tough, especially near the end." Carlita patted his arm. "When she cleans the whole house, she's getting close. I do know that."

Tony shoved his hands in his pockets. "No kidding. She called earlier and told me she was cleaning the kitchen cupboards."

"It won't be long now. I hope she hangs on long enough for the baby shower."

"I think she will," Tony said. "After that, all bets are off."

Back home, Carlita fixed a cup of tea and flipped through the bookie journal again, stopping when she found the entry with Cray's name.

Thinking it wouldn't hurt to do a little digging around, she logged onto the home computer and tried finding the name "Cray" to no avail. Her stomach grumbled, and she realized she hadn't given a single thought about what to make for dinner.

"Let's see what we can find, Rambo." Carlita began rummaging around in the fridge, which is where Pete found her when he and Gunner arrived.

"I brought dinner."

"Oh, good. I was wondering what to fix," Carlita said.

He lifted the to-go bag. "Tonight we're dining on French onion soup and toasted club sandwiches."

"Sounds good."

"Soup is for the birds," Gunner squawked. "Where's Snitch?"

"He's been asking for you-know-who all day," Pete sighed. "One of us must have mentioned her name."

"Gunner misses his gal."

Elvira had brought Snitch over not long after she adopted the parrot, concerned because she was showing signs of stress or depression. As soon as Gunner and Snitch met, it was an instant and mutual attraction. The visit had worked wonders and helped pull the parrot out of her funk.

Although Carlita and Elvira planned for the two to get together again, it hadn't happened yet. "Maybe I can give Elvira a call to see if she wants to bring S-N-I-T-C-H over."

"Snitch. Where is Snitch?" Gunner's head bobbed up and down, peering through the bars, searching for his love.

"Let me see what I can do, Gunner." Carlita stepped out onto the balcony and closed the door behind her. She called Elvira's office first, only to find out she wasn't there. She tried her cell phone next.

A breathless Elvira answered. "Hey, Carlita. Were your ears burning? I was wondering how your visit with Cool Bones went."

"He's down in the dumps. He told us what happened the last time he saw Rudy McCoy." Carlita mentioned the bookie journal. "Cool Bones must not remember, but he specifically wrote about meeting Cray."

"Interesting. Is there anything you need from me?"

"Not yet. I'll let you know." Carlita glanced toward the living room. Gunner was still pacing, his head bobbing up and down. "Gunner has been asking for Snitch."

"You want to set up another date?"

"Sure. What about tomorrow?"

"Tomorrow?"

Carlita warmed to the idea. "You'll be gone all day knocking out your court-ordered punishment."

"I've been trying to figure out what to do with Snitch while I'm on trash patrol. She would love to see Gunner again." Elvira's voice grew muffled as she baby talked her parrot. "She's on a new kick."

"What kind of kick?"

"You'll find out soon enough. It's annoying."

"What if Gunner picks it up?"

"I hope not."

"Maybe this isn't such a good idea."

"You can't back out now. Snitch heard us talking and is asking for Gunner. She'll be heartbroken."

"Fine," Carlita relented. "You can bring Snitch over in the morning before you report to the police department."

"We'll swing by around seven thirty. I'll be sure to bring some of her favorite toys. See you tomorrow."

"Wait." It was too late. Elvira was gone.

Carlita stared at the phone. "I hope I didn't just create a lot of stress and headache for myself."

She slipped back inside and motioned to Pete. "I have some news."

"About visitors?"

"Yeah." Carlita pulled him toward her. "Elvira is bringing Snitch over tomorrow morning at seven thirty," she whispered in his ear. "Fair warning. Apparently, she's picked up some sort of habit or words Elvira isn't thrilled about."

"Uh-oh."

"Uh-oh is right. She wouldn't tell me what it was. It's too late now."

"Snitch is here. Snitch is here," Gunner crowed.

"Have you ever noticed Gunner has excellent hearing?" Pete joked.

"Something tells me tomorrow will be interesting." Carlita mentioned the bookie journal and her promise to deliver it to Cool Bones.

"I can take it down to the station."

"I have a better idea. Elvira can take it with her when she drops her feathered friend off." Carlita poured sodas while Pete warmed their soup.

After finishing, the couple carried their dinner out to the terrace. Despite the warm summer temps, a gentle breeze blew, making it more bearable.

"I love this rooftop terrace," Carlita said. "Even in the middle of summer, we're up high enough to catch a nice breeze."

"And it's even better spent with you." Pete grasped Carlita's hand and kissed the top. "This year has gone by fast."

Carlita stirred her soup. "It has. Do you think it's time to start seriously thinking about stepping back from the daily grind?"

Pete considered her question. "Maybe. You're fortunate enough to have Tony and Mercedes already helping. Passing the reins will be easy. I, on the other hand, do not think Kristine is interested in inheriting or running a pirate ship or restaurant."

"We also have the excavation downstairs," Carlita reminded him. "Who knows how long the project will drag on."

Although moving at a slow pace, the hunt for treasure and what might be buried in Pete's basement was moving forward. Tedious, delicate work to ensure potential artifacts weren't destroyed was the goal.

The slow progress was causing Elvira to lose interest. Hence, her trip to Alaska.

"Let's do this. Let's wait until the project wraps up. I wouldn't mind doing some traveling." Carlita sipped her soup. "A cruise with Millie on board Siren of the Seas sounds fun."

"I've heard so much about Millie and her friends." Pete reached for his sandwich. "Why don't we take a look at the ship's itinerary and plan a cruise?"

"Seriously?" Carlita clasped her hands. "I would love to take another cruise."

The couple discussed the idea, and Carlita promised to check out upcoming voyages.

Dinner cleanup was easy-breezy, and the rest of the evening was quiet and peaceful. The couple turned in early, knowing the following day would be a busy one.

As soon as Carlita's head hit the pillow, she was fast asleep.

*****

Having had a good night's rest, Carlita was up and out of bed early the next morning. She fixed a pot of coffee and dressed for the day.

At exactly seven thirty on the dot, the outer bell rang. Carlita ran down to let Elvira in. She opened the door and found her former neighbor and tenant with a birdcage in hand.

On closer inspection, she noticed Elvira's face was pale and her hair matted, as if she'd just crawled out of bed. "What happened to you?"

"We overslept. I didn't have time to shower. I forgot to pack Snitch's food."

"No worries. We have plenty of food." Carlita led Elvira up the stairs and into the living room.

"Snitchy Snitch." Snitch announced her arrival.

Gunner, who was near the door, excitedly flapped his wings. "Gunner is handsome."

Back and forth, the parrots bantered, chattering nonstop.

"She's getting kinda picky about what she eats," Elvira warned. "The only thing I can get her to eat are bell peppers, apples and raw broccoli."

"We have plenty," Carlita promised.

"I hate to drop and run, but I promised Mercedes I would meet her at the PD at ten 'til."

"While you're there." Carlita grabbed Cool Bones' bookie journal off the counter. "Can you take this to the visitor's desk? I put a sticky note on top with Cool Bones' name so they know who to give it to."

Elvira snapped to attention and saluted her. "Will do."

"Thanks, and good luck."

"Mercedes and I might need it," Elvira said. "I mentioned to a friend I was doing trash pickup for community service and he laughed his head off."

"Why was he laughing?"

"When I asked him what was so funny, he told me I would find out soon enough. Gotta run." Elvira dashed out, leaving in such a hurry she forgot to tell Snitch goodbye.

Fortunately, the bird didn't seem to notice. She only had eyes for Gunner.

"Gunner is enchanted," Pete said.

"I would say the same about Snitch." Carlita found a bell pepper in the fridge and began slicing it. She sliced an apple and split the food up, placing even amounts on two plates before sliding them into their respective cages.

Snitch scooted across the bar. She cocked her head and belted out, "vamos a bailar!"

"What in the world?"

"She sounds like she's in pain," Pete said.

Snitch repeated the phrase, this time even louder, causing Carlita to plug her ears. "This must be what Elvira was talking about."

"It's a horrible, shrieking sound." Pete frowned.

Rambo scrambled to his feet and ran out of the room, desperate to escape the racket.

"We need to figure out how to distract her." Carlita grimaced. "If not, something tells me we're in for a very long day."

Chapter 11

Mercedes stepped off the curb, her hands on her hips, watching Elvira scurry along the sidewalk. "I was beginning to think you packed your bags and fled Savannah to escape our punishment."

"Nah. I took Snitch to your mother's place this morning so she could spend some time with Gunner. She asked me to drop Cool Bones' bookie journal off at the visitor's center for him."

"How cute. Snitch and Gunner are having a date day."

"Dernice is filling in for me, which means Snitch would have been home alone. She was geeked when she saw Gunner."

"Parrots in love." Mercedes sucked in a breath, eyeing the front of the police station. "I'm ready to get this trash-picking project over with. I'm hoping to be home by five so I can get ready for Shelby's baby shower."

"You and me both." Elvira reached for the door handle. "We'll suck it up and get the job done."

"It is kind of funny if you think about it. Besides, how bad can it be?" Mercedes stepped inside and followed the arrow for community service attendees.

The hall zigged and zagged, turning left and then sharply to the right. A sign stand pointed left. As she and Elvira drew closer, Mercedes could hear muffled voices.

Stepping into a large open room, they found a check-in desk surrounded by floor-to-ceiling metal lockers, the kind you found in elementary schools. What appeared to be changing rooms lined the far wall.

Mercedes, with Elvira by her side, joined the back of the line, furtively studying the people ahead of her. A young kid who couldn't have been more than sixteen. A woman covered in tattoos, sporting black and purple-colored hair, stood behind him.

The line moved at a brisk pace. As they drew closer, she noticed the clerk handing out orange outfits. Mercedes nudged Elvira. "She's handing out orange jumpsuits," she whispered.

"Great." Elvira rolled her eyes. "Orange is my least favorite color, not to mention it washes out my skin tone and makes me look sick."

"We might not have a choice."

They reached the front of the line. Mercedes offered the woman a half-hearted smile. "Good morning. Mercedes Garlucci reporting for cleanup."

"Mercedes Garlucci." The woman ran her pen along the list. "I don't see your name."

"Seriously?" She leaned in. "Maybe the judge changed his mind."

Elvira nudged her aside. "Check for me. Elvira Cobb."

"Elvira Cobb. Yes. I see you here. What size jumpsuit do you need?" The woman lifted her gaze, sizing Elvira up. "Triple XL?"

"Triple XL?" Elvira gasped. "No way. I'm an XL all day long."

The clerk grabbed an orange outfit from the rack. "The dressing rooms are over there. After you've changed, place your belongings in a locker. Don't lose the key. There's a twenty-five dollar charge if you lose it."

Elvira snatched the jumpsuit off the counter and shifted to the side. "What about her?" She jabbed her finger at Mercedes. "She's the reason I'm in this pickle. If she's skating out of community service, so am I."

"If you walk out of here, the judge will issue a warrant for your arrest and put you back in jail," the clerk warned.

"This is so unfair," Elvira mumbled under her breath.

"Let me check again." The clerk cleared her throat, slowly running her finger down the list. "There you are. At the very bottom. Mercedes Garlucci. What size do you need, honey? You look like you could fit into a small."

"Maybe. To be safe, give me a medium, just in case."

"You got it." Humming under her breath, the woman took a medium outfit from the shelf and set it on the counter. "Good luck."

Mercedes thanked her and followed Elvira to the dressing rooms. "She was nice."

"To you. 'Good luck,'" she mimicked. "The woman needs customer/client training."

Mercedes gave her the side eye. "She wasn't mean to you. She was just being honest and told you what would happen if you skipped out."

"It didn't sound like a threat? Because it sure sounded like a threat to me. Oh well. I'm not here to make friends." Elvira disappeared into an empty changing room while Mercedes found another empty one two doors down.

She undressed and carefully folded her clothes before slipping the jumpsuit on. Critically eyeing her reflection, she tugged on the baggy waistline. Not wanting to bother the clerk and swap it out for a smaller size, Mercedes rolled the pant legs up, exited the changing room, and trekked over to the lockers.

Elvira had already finished storing her belongings and stood waiting for her near the door. "We better get a move on. I heard someone say the bus is already out front waiting for us."

"Bus?"

"Prison bus I'm guessing." Elvira shrugged. "I'm sure we'll find out soon enough."

Moving at a brisk clip, the women exited the building. A guard stood near the door. He directed them to the other side of the parking lot where an old yellow school bus sat idling.

Emblazoned on the side in bold black letters was *Savannah-Burnham Corrections Department*.

Mercedes shaded her eyes. "I can check riding on a prison bus off my bucket list."

"Seriously?" Elvira coughed loudly. "Who puts riding on a prison bus on their bucket list? What's next...armed robbery?"

"Kidding. I'm kidding." Mercedes reluctantly reached for the handrail and climbed the steps. The front row seats were already occupied. Midway back, she found an available seat and settled in.

Elvira dropped down across from her. "I wonder where they're taking us."

"The judge mentioned the streets and squares, so I'm pretty sure we're staying downtown."

Finally, the last prisoner...err...community service attendee boarded and off they went. The bus jostled out of the parking lot and onto the street.

Although the windows were tinted, Mercedes could see they were heading toward the riverfront district. Passing by familiar blocks, they cruised past the Parrot House Restaurant and turned onto Bay Street before pulling into Morrell Park's parking lot.

"We could have walked here," Elvira muttered.

"Right?" Mercedes noticed pedestrians...joggers, walkers and tourists congregating off to the side, watching the bus grind to a halt. "Great. We have an audience."

"I hope no one recognizes us," Elvira said.

"How embarrassing would it be to run into a Ravello's customer?"

Whoosh. Engaging the air brakes, the driver shut the engine off and slid the door open. The uniformed officer seated at the front was the first to exit. He stood near the bottom step.

"Time to go, folks," the driver announced.

Mercedes followed the others along the narrow aisle, making her way to the front of the bus and down the steps.

The uniformed officer waited until the final passenger appeared. Standing ramrod straight, he spoke. "My name is Officer Kean! You will address me as such at *all* times! You are here to work and work...you...will!"

With hands folded behind his back, he strode in front of them. "If you even so much as look at me wrong, I will report your misconduct to the judge. Even though you are only here for the day, keep in mind I have the power to have you thrown back in jail. Do I make myself clear?"

Stunned silence ensued, followed by a few half-hearted, "Yes, sir."

Keane walked the length of the lineup, staring each of his wards down. "I said...do I make myself clear?"

Elvira snapped to attention and saluted him. "Yes, sir!" she belted out.

The officer's eyes narrowed. "Are you mocking me?"

"N-no." Her eyes grew round as saucers. "I would never do that, your excellency."

Mercedes groaned inwardly, silently urging Elvira to shut up.

Much to her relief, Kean appeared not to take offense. "Now get your sorry butts to work and don't let me hear a peep out of any of you."

The driver handed out clear plastic garbage bags and rubber gloves. "We'll be splitting up into groups. The first group will cover the far end of the park. A second group will remove trash from the center while the final group will clean the area over by the ferry dock."

Kean picked up. "I anticipate finishing early, which means we'll return to the bus and head over to the squares. In other words, each of you *will* put in a full eight hours of community service."

As luck would have it, Kean was in charge of Mercedes and Elvira's group. He directed them to the swanky high-rise hotel on the east end.

Mercedes swooped down and grabbed an empty water bottle. She found the missing cap a few feet away. A crumpled soda can and fast food wrapper were nearby. "This reminds me of the inside of your van," she joked.

"What's wrong with my van?"

"Nothing other than it looks like you live in it."

"Very funny." Elvira lagged behind, swooping and scooping at a much slower speed. At one point, their group leader must've noticed her lollygagging and told her to pick up the pace.

Her cheeks turned beet red. For a second, Mercedes thought she was going to snap back. Instead, she wisely kept her mouth shut.

The cool morning air gave way to the scorching summer sun. Beads of sweat formed on Mercedes' brow. She swiped at them, trying not to focus on the fact that the cotton jumpsuit was clinging to her body in some extremely awkward spots.

"This is brutal."

She glanced over her shoulder and found Elvira hunched over, making a gagging sound.

Dropping her garbage bag on the ground, she rushed over. "Are you okay?"

"This has to be the most disgusting job on the planet."

"Don't think about it and keep moving." Mercedes said.

Officer Kean must've noticed the workers struggling. He called for a bathroom and a water break. As soon as they finished, they began working their way toward the bus, picking up a few scraps of trash they had missed on the first sweep.

The second group was already there, while the third and final group caught up with them a short time later.

Mercedes hung back, letting the others board first. Already overheated, the longer she put off boarding the sweltering bus, the better.

Which worked out fine until she discovered her former seat was occupied. Not a fan of the "back of the bus," she opted for the seat adjacent to Officer Kean, directly behind the driver.

"Where are we heading next, boss?" the driver asked.

"City Market and the surrounding squares. A festival is starting this weekend. We want it to look clean and pretty for the visitors."

"You got it." The driver revved up the engine and the bus rumbled off down the road.

Mercedes leaned her head against the seat and closed her eyes. Her punishment would soon be over. At least she wasn't Cool Bones, stuck in jail with a murder charge hanging over his head.

"...Thirsty Crow."

She perked up when she heard Officer Kean mention the bar.

"...tough deal," he said. "I've heard Cool Bones and the Jazz Boys. They're good, one of the best bands around."

The driver glanced in the rearview mirror. "Our new cold case detective is on it. Heard they got something solid on Cool Bones."

"Eh." Kean shrugged. "I'm not so sure it's a slam dunk. They might not be done digging up bodies, at least that's what I'm hearing."

"You mean Cool Bones might not be the one?"

"It's possible." Kean shot Mercedes a side glance, realizing she was listening in. He abruptly changed the subject.

Before she could think of something to say, to keep the conversation going, they reached their destination, Freedom Square, which was smack-dab in the center of Savannah's tourist district.

Officer Kean exited the bus and waited for them to assemble on the sidewalk. He repeated his previous instructions...wash, rinse, and repeat. In other words, grab a trash bag and start swooping and scooping.

Elvira worked her way toward Mercedes, who was picking up trash around the square's perimeter. "I noticed you cozying up to the cop on the way over here."

"I wasn't cozying up." Mercedes filled her in on the conversation. "We drove by Thirsty Crow and he and the driver started talking about Cool Bones' arrest. We need to get the scoop."

"How?"

"I have an idea. It'll have to wait until we're on our way back." Mercedes gathered up a handful of trash surrounding the trash bin. "How lazy is this? They couldn't be bothered to toss the trash in the can."

"Pigs." Elvira shook her head in disgust. "You know what I found over by the Waving Girl statue?"

"Hard telling."

"Used toilet paper."

Mercedes' eyes widened in horror. "Gross."

"Right? It made me gag."

"I figured it was the heat." Mercedes dropped a crumpled water bottle in her bag. "The good news is we'll be done in a few hours."

Elvira abruptly stopped. "Great. Don't look now, but we have company."

Chapter 12

Mercedes swiped her sweaty forehead, her heart plummeting when Sam and his tour group rounded the corner, strolling right toward them.

"Duck." She scooted behind the trash can. It was too late. Sam had spotted her.

With a pep in his step, he made a beeline for the square.

Elvira clutched her bag of trash and greeted him with a friendly, "Hey, Sam."

"Hello, Elvira." Sam stopped his group only a few feet away from the women. "I'm stopping for a minute to introduce you to a fine group of helpers who are working with the Savannah-Burnham Police Department to keep our city streets clean."

A woman smirked, giving Mercedes the once over. "They look like inmates to me."

"Not inmates. More like reformed citizens."

A man, clutching a tour guide map, forced his way to the front. "I'm having trouble hearing. What did you say?"

Sam grabbed his bullhorn. "Can you hear me now?"

"Yes," the group replied in unison.

"Perfect." Sam proudly pointed to Mercedes. "In fact, one of them is none other than my girlfriend, Mercedes. She's doing her part to clean up the community, right, babe?!"

The crowd started laughing.

Mercedes could feel the tips of her ears burn. Never in all her life had she felt so humiliated. She was sweaty. She was thirsty. She was tired and now she was being laughed at.

Furious, Mercedes shot him a death look. "Jerk," she gritted through clenched teeth.

Sam lowered the bullhorn, a confused expression on his face. "I thought you would appreciate a shout-out."

"You're an idiot," she fumed.

"I-I'm sorry. I didn't mean to make you mad." Sam apologized and hurriedly ushered his tour group out of the area.

Officer Kean wandered over. "You and Sam Ivey are friends?"

"Not anymore." Mercedes blew air through thinned lips. "He made a fool out of me."

Kean tilted his head. "You know what? I thought your name sounded familiar. You and your family own the Italian restaurant over in Walton Square."

"Ravello's Italian Eatery."

"I think you've waited on me before. I have never had a bad meal there."

Mercedes' heart skipped a beat. This was her chance to invite Kean, who knew something about

Cool Bones' case, to the restaurant to glean more information about what evidence the authorities had.

"We're planning on offering first responders free meals this Wednesday," Mercedes fibbed. "Would you be interested in stopping by?"

"A free meal?" Kean's eyes lit. "I can't recall if Ravello's serves any southern dishes. I love southern food."

"I...uh. As a matter of fact, my mother has been working on a new recipe. Biscuits and gravy."

"There's nothing tastier than a plate full of biscuits and gravy." He smacked his lips. "I'm getting hungry just thinking about it."

"As soon as we get back on the bus, I'll write you up a coupon. All you'll need to do is present it to the server. Or...if you can make it between eleven and three, I'll be working."

"I'm sure I can fit it into my schedule. I'll be looking forward to it." He thanked Mercedes before leaving to check on his other charges.

Elvira slipped in next to her. "Slick move. He walked right into it."

"Yep. Hopefully, I can talk Ma into whipping up a batch of her biscuits and gravy." Mercedes placed a light hand on her lower back, now sending out warning twinges. "We better get back to stooping and scooping."

The afternoon wore on, and Mercedes was shocked by the amount of trash. Soda cans, empty water bottles, discarded downtown maps, store receipts.

At four o'clock on the dot, Kean announced they would start wrapping things up and head back to the bus.

The minutes dragged by. Elvira began moving at a snail's pace, her complexion blotchy and red.

Mercedes saw her stumble and hurried over. "Are you okay?"

"I'm getting too old for all this bending and stooping," she groaned.

"Rest for a minute. I'll finish cleaning your area." Despite being exhausted, Mercedes picked up the pace, collecting the remaining trash.

Out of the corner of her eye, she caught a flit of movement. It was Dernice, jogging across Freedom Square, heading right toward them.

"What's my sister doing here?" Elvira shaded her eyes and shifted the bag of trash to her other hand.

"I have no idea."

A breathless Dernice caught up with them. "Hey, Elvira, Mercedes. I was hoping I would catch you," she gasped. "I finished your security job over at the convention center. How's it going?"

"It sucks. I'm exhausted, hungry, thirsty and cranky," Elvira complained.

Dernice's brows furrowed. "Your face is red. This'll work out perfectly."

Elvira stared at her. "What will work out perfectly?"

"Remember how you said you needed a catchy slogan to attract new clients? I got to thinking about it and realized a golden opportunity has been dropped into our laps."

"Golden opportunity?" Mercedes echoed.

"For a catchy ad." Dernice pulled her cell phone from her pocket. "Stand over next to the trash can with your bag of trash."

"You have lost your mind," Elvira snapped. "I am in no mood to have my picture taken."

"It'll only take a second." Dernice waved her phone in the air. "Hear me out. This is the perfect setup. We can print new business cards with your picture and the slogan, 'Serving your community.' It's perfect."

Noting the murderous expression on Elvira's face and certain her sister was pushing her toward the breaking point, Mercedes stepped in between them. "As much as I applaud your creativity, now is not the time. It's been a long day and we're both exhausted."

"Which fits in perfectly with being a hard-working blue-collar worker," Dernice said. "I thought you would love the idea."

"Leave before the cops throw me back in jail for kicking your butt," Elvira growled.

"Dang. You're testy." Dernice started to say something else.

Mercedes grasped her arm, propelling her out of striking distance. "You should go."

"Fine." Dernice stalked off, but not before throwing another verbal jab her sister's way.

"Kean is coming." Mercedes and Elvira got back to work, clearing the corner quadrant.

"It's a wrap, ladies. Nice job. Even for you, Cobb."

"I tried my best...Sir," Elvira said.

Mercedes dropped her bag of trash in the bin and trudged back to the bus. Elvira flopped down on the seat. She leaned her head on the seat in front of her and closed her eyes.

Mercedes patted her shoulder. "You did good. You were a real trooper. Thank you."

"You're welcome. I'm looking forward to a nice, cool shower, to kick my feet up and plow through a pepperoni pizza."

The City Market was only a couple of blocks away from the downtown police department, and within a few short minutes, they were back in the parking lot. The cleaning crew quickly vacated the bus.

Mercedes lingered, letting the others off first. She caught up with Officer Kean, who stood at the bottom of the steps holding a clipboard. He handed her his pen. "Sign on the dotted line. You're free to leave after you return the work uniform."

"Thanks." Mercedes took the pen and signed her name. "Are you still interested in the southern-style biscuits and gravy meal at Ravello's tomorrow?"

"Yes, ma'am. I'm so hungry I could eat a bucketful."

"I'm not sure if Ma will have a bucketful for you. You said you thought you could make it between eleven and three?"

"I can."

"Then I won't bother writing a coupon. You can just ask for me."

"Mind if I bring a friend along?"

"Not at all. If your friend is a first responder, they're eligible for a free meal. It is on a trial basis, so until Ma rolls it out, I wouldn't tell too many people," Mercedes warned.

Kean made a zipping motion across his lips. "Not a peep. See you then."

She ran inside, grabbed her things from the locker and swapped out the jumpsuit for her street clothes. She dropped the soiled outfit in the bin and tracked down Elvira, who was sitting on the bench out front.

"You look like I feel," Mercedes said. "Why don't I give Ma a call to see if she can swing by and pick us up?"

Toot. Toot. An EC Security Services van cruised into the parking lot and pulled alongside the curb. Dernice rolled the window down. "Need a lift?"

"Your timing is impeccable." Elvira limped to the passenger side and slid in while Mercedes climbed into the back. "Thanks for picking us up."

"You're welcome. It's my way of making amends for earlier."

"Well played," Elvira said. "I almost forgive you for coming up with the harebrained idea of using my punishment for an ad."

"I'm still not giving up. In fact, I'm having a mockup done in case you change your mind." Dernice told them she ran into Sam, who had snapped a photo of Elvira and Mercedes in action.

"He did not," Mercedes gasped.

"He most definitely did," Dernice said. "He sent a copy to all of us in a group text."

Mercedes muttered under her breath. "He's not scoring any brownie points."

"I gotta say...you looked pretty good. Better than Elvira."

"Of course she looked better," Elvira grunted. "She wasn't the one who had to pick up poop."

Dernice's jaw dropped. "You picked up poop?"

"Toilet tissue with brown remnants. What do you think?"

"It could have been worse."

The sisters bickered all the way to Walton Square, disagreeing about how much worse community service could have been.

Mercedes was relieved it was over. She had knocked out two things. Putting the community service behind her *and* finding a police department employee who might have information that could help them clear Cool Bones' name.

She needed to make sure her mother would have time to whip up the special dish. But first, she had a baby shower to host.

Chapter 13

Carlita finished filling the platter with mini meatballs and placed them next to the prosciutto-wrapped avocado bites. She set the sheet cake and paper plates off to the side and did a final check of the gift table.

The apartment door flew open. A weary Mercedes trudged inside. "Hey, Ma. Sorry if I'm late."

Carlita tied the bouquet of balloons to the guest of honor's chair. "How did it go?"

"About as good as can be expected." Mercedes plopped down on the sofa and kicked her shoes off. "Except for the fact Sam brought his tour group by to introduce me to them."

"Introduce you?"

"Fully clothed in an orange jumpsuit with a prison guard standing nearby." Mercedes placed her head in her hands. "I've never been so embarrassed in my life."

Carlita chuckled, envisioning the look on her daughter's face when Sam showed up. "I saw a picture of you and Elvira in action. Where were you?"

"City Market. Smack dab in the middle of the square. He humiliated me on purpose," Mercedes said.

"The City Market is part of his tour route," her mother reminded her.

"It is, and it would have been fine had he not introduced me via his bullhorn."

"I wish I could've been there. At least he isn't embarrassed at the thought of his girlfriend performing community service. I call it devotion."

Mercedes lifted her head, trying to visualize how she must've looked. "I suppose. He didn't seem at all shy about letting people know who I was. It wasn't so funny at the time."

"I bet you were fit to be tied." Carlita shook her finger. "You should give him the benefit of the doubt."

"I'll think about it." Mercedes changed the subject. "Before I forget, remind me later, after the shower, to talk to you about making another batch of biscuits and gravy tomorrow morning."

"Why?"

"For the prison guard/cop I invited to Ravello's, who might have information on Cool Bones' case."

Ting. Ting. The outer bell rang.

Carlita hurried to the door. "I hope guests aren't already showing up."

"I need to shower and change." Mercedes slowly stood.

"Go ahead. I'll see who it is." Carlita ran downstairs and found a delivery person standing on the stoop with a bouquet of flowers in hand. "I have a delivery for Mercedes Garlucci."

"Mercedes is my daughter." Carlita could barely see the man past the gigantic bouquet of long stemmed red roses. "Do you need me to sign?"

"Please." He handed her a clipboard.

Carlita signed her name and traded the clipboard for the bouquet. "These are stunning."

"It's our most extravagant bouquet. I don't know what the sender did, but he must've gotten into some pretty deep doo to spring for these flowers."

"He did. This should get him pretty far in making amends." Carlita thanked the delivery person and carried the bouquet back upstairs.

She placed them on the counter and texted Shelby to let her know they were ready for their special guest of honor.

Shelby and Violet arrived within minutes.

Carlita gave her daughter-in-law a gentle hug. "You're absolutely glowing."

"More like sweating." Shelby fanned her face. "The baby is making me hot."

"It won't be long now." Carlita hugged Violet next. "Are you ready to help Nana host the baby shower?"

"Yep." Violet twirled in a circle. "Mom bought me a new dress for the party."

"It's beautiful, like you."

Shelby waddled over to the counter. "These roses are gorgeous."

"They're Sam's apology roses for Mercedes." Carlita told her what had happened.

"Oh, boy." Shelby let out a low whistle. "I bet she was steaming."

"Steaming, stewing. Here she comes now."

Mercedes breezed into the living room, looking no worse for the wear, sporting pink shorts and a crisp white cotton blouse.

"Your mother told me what happened and how Sam showed up downtown," Shelby said. "I don't think I would have been happy either."

"I was ticked. He's lucky the cop was there, and I didn't punch him."

Carlita motioned to the flowers. "These were delivered a few minutes ago."

Her daughter's expression softened. "Someone sent me flowers?"

"I'm gonna go out on a limb and guess it was Sam. The biggest, most extravagant bouquet he could buy," Carlita said. "At least according to the delivery driver."

"I see an envelope." Mercedes tugged the envelope from the holder. She flipped the flap and removed the card. "Flowers for the most beautiful community service worker in Savannah. I'm sorry." The card was signed, *Love, Sam.*

"He must've realized how upset you were, and this is his way of apologizing."

"Your flowers are so pretty, Aunt Mercedes," Violet said.

"They are. I suppose I should thank him." She grabbed her cell phone and stepped out onto the balcony.

Shelby waited until the door closed. "Sam's been treading on thin ice lately, as far as Mercedes is concerned."

Carlita sighed. "She put him on long-term relationship probation, because of the whole Natalie incident."

"I can't say I blame her, but maybe it's time to forgive and forget or..."

"Move on," Carlita said.

"Yep."

The conversation ended when Mercedes returned. "Sam is home. He wants to know if I have a minute to stop by."

"Go ahead. We'll greet the guests if anyone shows up early." After she left, Carlita grabbed the special gift she'd purchased for Violet. "This is for you."

Violet's eyes grew round as saucers. "A present for me?"

"For being my special helper."

The young girl reached past the sparkly lavender tissue paper and removed a purple jumpsuit. Along with the jumpsuit were hair bows, matching purple sandals and a heart-shaped locket.

"You can save the outfit for another day since you're wearing your new dress."

Violet flung her arms around Carlita and hugged her tightly. "You're the best Nana ever."

"And you're the best granddaughter." Carlita blinked back the sudden tears, overcome by emotion and love for the young girl who had captured her heart. "Papa Pete...Gramps and I love you very much."

Mercedes reappeared, her cheeks flushed and clutching a sheet of paper. "Sam wanted to apologize in person and give me this."

"What is it?"

She handed it to her mother.

Carlita slipped her reading glasses on, skimming the hotel reservation for a swanky resort in Hilton Head.

"He booked us a romantic weekend getaway. He said I've been working too hard and could use a break."

"How sweet." Carlita handed it back. "Red roses, romantic getaways. Sam is a keeper."

"He's totally redeemed himself."

The outer bell rang. "It's time to celebrate Baby Garlucci." Carlita darted downstairs to welcome their guests. She escorted the women, friends of Shelby's, to the apartment and returned in time for another round of arrivals.

One after another, all bearing gifts for the mother-to-be. Soon, the apartment was packed. Cheerful voices. Smiling faces.

Working as a team, Carlita, Mercedes, and Violet hustled and hosted. Tons of food. Lots of laughter. There were games and gifts galore. A stroller, newborn outfits, baby blankets, diapers, rattles and even a bouncy seat. So many gadgets and gizmos, Carlita wondered where they would put it all. Fortunately, she had a very good idea. There was another big surprise she couldn't wait to share.

After the guests left, Carlita and Mercedes made several trips back and forth, helping Shelby carry the gifts to their cramped apartment at the other end of the alley.

"Where you gonna put all of this?" Mercedes asked.

"I wish I knew." Shelby sighed. "I forgot how much stuff babies need."

"I might have a solution." Carlita caught her daughter's eye when Shelby looked away and winked. "I haven't given you my gift yet. I want to wait until Tony is around to give it to you."

"You've already done so much," Shelby protested.

Carlita placed her hand on her big belly. "Believe me...you're going to love it. I promise."

"I'm sure we will. Thank you, Carlita and Mercedes. I couldn't ask for a better family."

"We feel the same." Mercedes hugged her sister-in-law.

With a final hug for Violet, Carlita and her daughter trekked out of the apartment. The baby shower was a wonderful break, a welcome break from worrying about Cool Bones.

Something told her they would need to double down on their efforts if they planned to make headway in helping their friend and tenant.

Chapter 14

"What time is the cop...guard...coming by?" Carlita began spooning the biscuit dough onto the cookie sheet.

"I told him Ravello's was serving your biscuits and gravy from eleven to three."

"You should've made it later to give me more time."

"I wanted to make sure I was working, so I could wait on his table. Once he's stuffed, we can swoop in and try to get the inside scoop."

"You're sure he knows something?"

"We happened to drive by the Thirsty Crow. The bus driver started talking about Cool Bones and what had happened. Officer Kean said something about it not being a slam dunk case and the investigators might not be done digging up bodies."

"So you're thinking we need to figure out what the cops are investigating?"

"If we can," Mercedes said. "Even if we can't, something tells me this Cray person is a person of interest."

"I was thinking about running by the apartment where Cool Bones met the guy," Carlita said. "I wonder if the landlady, Culpepper, is still around."

"She's around somewhere if she called the cops after recognizing Cool Bones."

Carlita got to work, whipping up a batch of creamy bacon gravy, enough for two people with leftovers to take home.

As soon as they finished, mother and daughter carried the dishes from Mercedes' apartment, down the alley and into the restaurant's kitchen.

Arnie, the manager, did a double take when he saw them. "Hey, Carlita, Mercedes."

"Hello, Arnie. We have a special customer coming in between eleven and three to sample a new dish."

"I remember you mentioning adding a southern dish to the menu. Is this it?"

"It is. I don't have enough to roll it out, at least not yet." Carlita plucked a bowl from the shelf, set a biscuit in the bottom, and poured a generous amount of gravy on top. "Would you do me a favor and try it?"

"I thought you'd never ask." Arnie grabbed a spoon and dug in. "This is delish. Nice and creamy, with a hint of rosemary."

"My secret Italian ingredient," Carlita said. "It doesn't taste bland?"

"Nope. It's perfect." He gave her a thumbs up. "Order the ingredients and as soon as they come in, we'll roll it out as a weekly special, or perhaps put it on our Sunday brunch menu."

"You read my mind. I figured we'll offer it as a special once a week to see how it goes," Carlita said. "If it takes off, we can add it to the regular menu."

Mercedes unfolded her work apron and slipped it over her head. She glanced at the clock. It was almost eleven. Officer Kean had four hours to claim his special meal. It was up to them to work their magic, to get him to spill the beans and share what he knew about Rudy McCoy's death.

Monitoring the front entrance, Mercedes got to work, taking orders, delivering cooked-to-order meals, and clearing dishes. During a break, she thought about Sam's flowers and his apology for embarrassing her. She told him she forgave him, but a small part of her was still upset about the incident.

It reminded her of other times, little jabs he'd made. To be fair, Sam had good qualities, and even some great qualities. He was always willing to help the Garluccis during times of trouble and turmoil.

Sam was hardworking, fun, funny, patient and kind. On the flip side, he had a hard edge. She suspected it was from years of working as a cop. He had never been unkind to Mercedes, but he had an unwavering, stubborn, and prideful side.

Maybe what the couple needed was time away, to figure out if they could work through some past resentments and finally decide if they had a future together. Hilton Head might be the perfect place to figure it out.

Two o'clock rolled around and Mercedes was beginning to think Officer Kean wouldn't show. At quarter past, she spotted him, along with another uniformed officer, standing near the hostess stand waiting to be seated.

Mercedes promptly assembled two glasses of ice water and made a beeline for their table. "Hello, Officer Kean."

"Hello, Mercedes Garlucci." He gave her the once over. "You clean up nicely."

163

"My work uniform is better than the orange jumpsuit," she joked.

"Much." He introduced his partner. "I've sold him on the biscuits and gravy."

"Ma made a special batch for you. Can I get you something to drink?"

"Sweet tea, if you have it."

"We do."

"Make it two," the other officer said.

"Coming right up." Mercedes hustled to the back. Her mother was at the computer, fiddling with the order screen. "They're here."

She stopped what she was doing. "The cop?"

"Yeah."

Carlita shoved her chair back. "While we were waiting, I figured it wouldn't hurt to make a batch of shrimp and grits to go along with the biscuits and gravy."

"It's free food. I'm sure they'll be thrilled with whatever we serve them." Mercedes swung by the beverage station to pour the sweet teas. She returned to the table and set them in front of the men. "Feel free to order off the menu if you change your mind."

"Not a chance." Kean closed his menu and set it aside. "I can taste the food already."

"Perfect. It shouldn't be long." Mercedes ran to the order screen and entered it in the system. While she waited, she checked on her other tables, making her rounds.

Thinking the special dishes were almost ready to go, she returned to the kitchen and found her mother standing at the prep counter. "I'm plating the food now."

"Awesome. I was thinking we could deliver it together, so you can meet Officer Kean and maybe mention Cool Bones."

"Sounds good." Carlita filled two plates with shrimp and grits and two more with a generous portion of the main meal. "We're ready to roll."

Mercedes carried the order into the dining room. She unfolded the tray stand and placed the tray on top. "Ma made shrimp and grits to go with the other dish."

"Shrimp and grits?" Officer Kean eagerly eyed the food. "This might become my new favorite restaurant."

Mercedes introduced Carlita. "This is my mother, Carlita Garlucci Taylor."

"How do you do?" Carlita shook hands with the men. "My daughter said you treated her well yesterday. Thank you for watching over her."

"She was a good sport about it. The other woman she was with...Elvira..."

"Cobb," Carlita said.

"Elvira Cobb was a pain in the butt. The woman whined about everything."

"She was having a hard time keeping up," Mercedes said. "I know by the end of the day she was exhausted."

"With any luck, she learned her lesson and won't ever see me again." Kean reached for his silverware. "This looks delicious."

"I hope you enjoy the biscuits and graves." Carlita nearly dropped the dish of food. "Did I...uh...say biscuits and graves? I meant biscuits and gravy."

Mercedes handed them extra napkins. "Can I get you anything else?"

"No. I think we're fine. In fact, we're mighty fine," Kean said.

"Enjoy." Mercedes followed her mother out of the dining room. They hovered near the server station, watching the men dig in. "We'll get them nice and full before we start asking questions."

"Did you hear what I said?" Carlita smacked her forehead. "Biscuits and graves."

"Freudian slip," Mercedes teased. "You were thinking about the grave, not gravy."

"Let's give them time to eat." Carlita ran back to the kitchen to finish her inventory order.

Meanwhile, Mercedes continued her rounds. She kept close tabs on the men, checking on them once and then waiting until they were almost done with their meal to return with two full to-go boxes.

"Ma boxed up some extras for you to take home." Mercedes set the containers on the table. "I take it you enjoyed the food?"

"This is the best meal I've had in a very long time," Kean said.

"Same here." His partner patted his stomach. "Those biscuits melted in my mouth. My mom used to make biscuits and gravy. It tasted very close to this. She was born and raised in South Georgia and was one of the best cooks on the planet."

"I've never had an offender offer me a free meal." Officer Kean clipped his radio to his belt.

"Picking up trash wasn't a ton of fun, but I could think of worse things to do."

"At least the judge didn't give you dumpster duty."

"Dumpster duty?" Mercedes made a choking sound. "I'm almost afraid to ask."

"It involves working at the local solid waste facility, sorting through recycle bins. If you're lucky, they put you in the hazardous waste section."

Mercedes shuddered. "I guess trash pickup was one of the preferred punishments."

"None of them are great," Kean said. "I hope I don't see you again working community service."

"I hope not either. I know this probably doesn't matter to you, but for the record, I didn't throw the beer bottle at Officer Perkins the other night at the Thirsty Crow."

A look of surprise flickered across Kean's face. "You were one of those who was arrested at the downtown bar?"

Carlita, who had stepped in next to her, spoke. "My daughter and her friends were there supporting Cool Bones and the Jazz Boys. Cool Bones is a tenant of ours."

"He's a good guy," Kean said. "I've been an admirer of the band for years."

"We don't believe he killed Rudy McCoy," Carlita added. "Mercedes and I visited Cool Bones in jail the other day. He swears it wasn't him. I believe him."

"Ma'am. I can't talk about the case," Kean said. "I'm not a part of the investigation."

"I understand. However, there is a person of interest Cool Bones mentioned. A man who goes by the name Cray."

"Cray," Kean repeated. "I'm not familiar with the case. Surely, Cool Bones has mentioned it to the authorities."

"He has. To be blunt, according to him, the investigators don't seem interested," Carlita said. "Do you have any suggestions on how we might help?"

Officer Kean glanced around. "I like you, Mrs. Taylor, and Mercedes. You seem like good, honest, hard-working people."

"We are. We also believe in justice and would like nothing more than to see Cool Bones exonerated."

"I do have a suggestion for you, a way to help him."

Chapter 15

Carlita held her breath. The free meals were going to pay off. "How can we help Cool Bones?"

"By staying out of the investigation. If the lead investigator catches wind you're poking around, he won't be happy." Officer Kean lifted the to-go container. "I will thoroughly enjoy eating this later tonight. Thanks again."

"You're welcome." Carlita waited until they were gone. "What a total waste of time."

"Maybe not." Mercedes flung her arm around her mother's shoulder. "The good news is, if I ever have to do community service again and Officer Kean is in charge, I'll get VIP treatment."

*****

Carlita wrapped up her shift and walked home. She found Pete seated at the counter; an array of papers spread out in front of him. "How did it go?"

"It was a big fat nothing burger. The cop took the food...literally ate the bait. He knew about Cool Bones' case. The only advice he gave us was to stay out of it."

"Which means you're back to square one."

"Almost back to square one," Carlita corrected. "Mercedes heard them saying something about digging up another grave. I think the next step is to swing by the apartment where it all went down, try to get a lay of the land and see if Mrs. Culpepper is still there."

"Cool Bones is lucky to have a friend like you," Pete said.

"Friends like us," she corrected

"Snitchy Snitch," Snitch said.

Carlita dropped her purse on the counter. "Gunner and Snitch are still chattering and catching up?"

"Nonstop. I had to leave for a couple of hours. When I got back, they were still at it."

Vamos a bailar! Snitch yelled.

"What does vamos a bailar mean?" Carlita asked.

"I have no idea." Pete shook his head. "I think she's speaking Spanish."

"I'm gonna look it up." Carlita grabbed her laptop. "I wonder how it's spelled."

"It sounds like vamoose and baylar," Pete said.

"That's what I was thinking." She typed in what they thought the parrot was saying and added "in Spanish," at the end. "The dictionary is suggesting vamos a bailar, which means let's dance."

"Maybe Elvira is teaching her some Spanish dance moves," Pete joked.

"There's only one way to find out." Carlita tracked down an online Spanish salsa playlist and hit the play button.

"Vamos a bailar." With tufted head bobbing, Snitch dipped and swayed, strutting along her post to the snappy tune. Maracas, timbales, a piano and conga drums filled the air, all in rhythm.

"Let's dance." Carlita clapped her hands and shimmied to the music.

"I thought you would never ask." Pete grabbed his wife's hand, spinning her around.

"Let's dance." Gunner, not to be left out, mimicked Snitch's moves.

Rambo pranced around, barking loudly.

The song ended, and Snitch stopped.

"Finito." Carlita laughed. "That was fun."

"I think we all did a fine job of cutting the rug." Pete tapped the top of his watch. "By the way, Elvira called. She should be here soon to pick Snitch up."

"I'm glad we offered to keep her. Something tells me it took some time for Elvira to recuperate from her community service." Pete leaned in and lowered his voice. "I think Snitch is spying on us. She keeps repeating what I say."

Carlita tapped her foot on the floor, studying the bird, who was watching them closely. "You think so?"

"I know so." Pete pulled a ten-dollar bill from his wallet. "I'll bet you ten bucks this bird is spying on us."

"Let's give her something to report back to Elvira." Carlita's expression grew mischievous. With her hands behind her back, she waltzed over to the bird's cage. "Hello, Snitch."

"Hello." Snitch tilted her head, studying Carlita. "Gunner is handsome."

"Gunner is handsome. Snitch is beautiful."

"Snitchy Snitch," the parrot replied.

"Tubby treasure."

"Tubby treasure," she repeated.

Pete chuckled, making his way over. "Don't forget—tubby treasure."

Buzz. Buzz. The bell rang. "I bet that's Elvira." Carlita ran downstairs to let her in.

"Hello, Elvira."

"Hey, Carlita." Elvira moved slowly, trudging up the stairs.

"Are you all right?"

"My back hurts. My legs ache. I think I got into some poison ivy." Elvira lifted her sleeve, revealing a huge red welt running down her arm. "I'm itching like crazy."

"I'm sorry to hear that." Carlita led her into the apartment.

"Intruder alert, intruder alert," Snitch screeched.

"Did you forget me already?" Elvira shook her head. "Ungrateful bird."

"Snitchy Snitch," Snitch said.

"Thanks for offering to keep her an extra day."

"You're welcome. It's been very...loud," Pete said. "Snitch is a good listener."

"And a great informant," Elvira snickered. "I hope you didn't say anything you wouldn't shout from the rooftops."

Carlita looked away, trying not to laugh. "Not that I can recall."

"I hate to grab and go, but I have a conference call with my contact in Alaska. I'm making final preparations for my trip."

"When is it?"

"The end of summer."

"Have you told Sharky you're coming?" Carlita asked.

"I mentioned it in passing. I want to surprise him. It's gonna be awesome."

"Are you sure he likes surprises?"

"Who doesn't love a good surprise? I mean…" Elvira struck a seductive pose and patted her hair. "He'll get all of this."

"Oh, brother." Carlita rolled her eyes. "Let us know when the date gets closer."

"You betcha." The trio discussed the progress of the basement dig and then Elvira left.

Suddenly, the apartment got very quiet. Gunner shuffled to the end of his perch. He tucked his head down and promptly fell asleep.

"Where did you come up with tubby treasure?" Pete asked.

"I don't know. It's the first thing that popped into my head and I figured it would be easy for Snitch to remember."

"Are you interested in betting on a timeline?" he asked.

"For Elvira to start looking for tubby treasure?" Carlita chuckled. "Less than 24 hours. She'll spend every free moment she has trying to figure it out."

Chapter 16

The apartment was quiet...almost too quiet...after Snitch and Elvira left.

"Snitch wore poor Gunner out," Carlita said.

"She wore me out too." Pete grabbed his keys. "I need to cover a manager's shift at the restaurant. What's on tap for the rest of your day?"

"I was thinking about checking in with Shelby to see if she needs anything." Carlita gave her husband a quick kiss. "I guess this means I'm on my own for dinner."

"Unfortunately. It's summer vacation season, which means the managers are all taking their breaks."

"Arnie will be taking his vacation soon too." Carlita accompanied Pete to the door and closed it behind him. She picked up her phone, intending to plug it into the charger, when she noticed she'd missed a call and text from Mercedes. *I'm at Steve's tattoo shop. Call me.*

She promptly dialed her daughter's number. "Hey, Mercedes."

"Hey, Ma. I stopped by Steve's shop. We got to talking about Cool Bones and the murder charges. You'll never guess who one of his tattoo customers is."

"Who?"

"Eunice Culpepper, Rudy McCoy's landlady, the woman who told investigators Cool Bones met with Rudy the day he died."

Carlita's mind whirled. "Steve knows Culpepper?"

"She's a regular customer."

"No kidding. I wonder if she still owns the apartment building."

"Steve looked her address up for me. She does, or at least she lives on the same street. Do you have time to swing by?"

"I have more than enough time to swing by. In fact, Pete's working which means I'm free as a bird for the rest of the day." Carlita promised she was on the way.

Thinking Rambo could use some fresh air and exercise, she tracked down her pup, who was sprawled out on the terrace deck, snoozing in the shade.

All it took was for Carlita to say the word "walk" and Rambo was on his feet, raring to go.

With keys and phone in hand, they hurried out of the apartment. To save time, they cut between the buildings, passing by *Colby's Corner Store* and Cricket Tidwell's *The Book Nook*, arriving at *Shades of Ink* within minutes.

Steve and Mercedes were there, along with Paisley.

Mercedes met her at the door. "That was fast. We were just talking about Mrs. Culpepper."

"She's a character," Paisley said. "A colorful character."

"Literally," Steve said. "She's what I call my bread-and-butter customer. We're working on a realism tattoo for her. They're complicated, which means I add more ink in stages."

"Realism tattoo?" Carlita echoed.

"Lifelike. The skin blends in with the artwork," Steve explained. "They're also pricey because of the time involved."

"Hers is a little." Paisley tipped her hand back and forth.

"Too realistic?"

"Dark. You would have to see it to understand it," Steve said. "Mercedes filled me in on what's going on. I have Culpepper's full address on file. If you have the street number, we can figure out if she's still living in the same apartment building."

"That would be great. Cool Bones remembered the exact address. I jotted it on a notepad and took a picture of the notes with my cell phone so I would have them with me." Carlita tracked down the picture and rattled off the address.

"Let's see what we have." Steve stepped behind the counter. "Culpepper has an appointment coming up for the next phase of her artwork."

"Maybe you could…"

"Pump her for information." Paisley finished Mercedes' sentence. "I was thinking the same thing."

"I got it," Steve said. "Her address is 2012 Gleason Street, Savannah, Georgia."

"It's a match. She still lives there. I think it's time to swing by and check it out." Carlita thanked him for looking it up.

"Cool Bones is my friend too. I hate seeing someone convicted of a crime they didn't commit. Especially a crime this serious."

Mercedes and Carlita began making their way to the door.

Paisley trailed behind. "Mind if I tag along?"

"The more the merrier." Carlita slipped her arm through Paisley's. "Maybe we'll get lucky and run into her while we're scoping the place out."

With a quick calculation and realizing Gleason Street was only a few blocks away, the trio decided to walk.

Over the years, Carlita and Mercedes had learned several shortcuts—how to get from one side of town to the other, bypassing the busy tourist districts and more popular squares.

While they walked, Carlita asked Paisley how she and Steve were doing. "Are you catching up on your past due bills?"

"Our utilities are all current. We're still behind on a couple of credit cards we've been using to stay afloat. Steve contacted the companies and we're hoping they'll work with us on a more manageable repayment plan."

"It never hurts to ask."

"Thank you for giving me a job and steady income," Paisley said. "If not for you, Steve and I would be out on the streets."

"No, you wouldn't," Carlita said. "We would find a way."

"Have you thought about a fundraiser?" Mercedes asked.

"We're barely scraping by. Fundraisers take money to make money."

"Not necessarily," Carlita said. "We could host something at Ravello's. Maybe include a silent auction. If we can get Cool Bones out of jail, I know he would help. I'll throw in some free food. Free music. I bet we could find plenty of donors."

"I like it." Paisley clapped her hands. "Or maybe we can host it at Steve's shop. When were you thinking?"

"We would need a month or so to plan it and send out invitations." Carlita tapped Paisley's arm. "It's up to you."

"You've already done so much for Steve and me. I hate to impose or cause more work."

Mercedes waved dismissively. "I love throwing parties and this would be for a good cause."

"A great cause," Carlita corrected.

"Let me text Steve." Paisley tapped out a short text. His reply was prompt. "He said if the Garluccis want to throw us a party, sign me up."

"I'll start working on it," Mercedes promised.

"I don't know what to say." Paisley blinked rapidly. "Your family has shown Steve and me nothing but kindness."

"We're returning the favor," Carlita said. "I'll never forget the day Mercedes and I rolled up in Walton Square. Steve was the first person to welcome us to the neighborhood."

"He helped us break into our own building," Mercedes reminded her.

"You're right. I forgot about that. It seems so long ago."

"We're getting close." Paisley slowed, studying the numbers on the front of the brownstone buildings. "These all look the same."

Carlita consulted her slip of paper. "This is the place."

"It's a little rough around the edges." Mercedes pointed to the weeds, choking out the bed of wildflowers lining the porch. The light fixture by the door was broken, exposing a bare light bulb.

The windows facing the street were missing screens. On closer inspection, Carlita noticed the one that still had a screen was ripped and torn. The sidewalk leading to the porch was covered with dirt and mold, in desperate need of a thorough cleaning.

"This place has seen better days," Mercedes whispered under her breath.

"Maybe Mrs. Culpepper is spending her lawn maintenance budget on tattoos," Carlita joked.

Paisley shaded her eyes and spun in a slow circle. "At least the apartment building blends in. So what's next?"

"I have a couple of ideas in mind. I noticed a surveillance camera pointed in our direction, which means I'm pretty sure we're being watched," Carlita said. "I'll figure out what to say if, or when, we meet Mrs. Culpepper. For now, follow my lead."

Chapter 17

Carlita veered left, picking her way through the overgrown grass.

Mercedes, with Paisley by her side, trailed behind, stopping when they reached the rear yard.

Compact and perfectly square, it was filled with the same overgrown grass. An unpaved alley ran along the back. To the right was a one-stall garage. The door hung haphazardly from its hinges, propped up by a cement block.

Off in the distance, a dog barked. Rambo, who was at Carlita's side, let out a warning growl, his ears pointing back.

"Rambo thinks this place is sketchy," Mercedes said.

"He's not the only one." Carlita inched forward, surveying their surroundings, and trying to recall exactly what Cool Bones had said about his last confrontation with Rudy McCoy. "According to Cool Bones, he met Rudy at his apartment. They stepped out into the backyard to discuss a customer. Rudy took a swing at him. Cool Bones knocked the guy to the ground and left not long after."

Mercedes walked to the edge of the alley. A chain-link fence, with missing sections and several bent posts separated the adjacent properties.

Paisley and Carlita made their way over. "What are you thinking?"

"I'm thinking the killer saw Cool Bones and Rudy argue. After Cool Bones left, he or she sneaked into Rudy's apartment and killed him."

"But not with the bat Cool Bones grabbed," Carlita reminded her. "The murder weapon was never found."

"What am I missing?" Paisley folded her arms. "The cops exhumed the guy's body. They found a fingerprint matching Cool Bones' print on the bat he was buried with, but it wasn't the murder weapon?"

"My guess is they believe it's evidence Cool Bones had access to a potential murder weapon." Carlita lifted a finger. "Number one, Culpepper saw them arguing shortly before Rudy's death. Secondly, they now have a matching print. Third, he has a criminal record, albeit only for minor stuff."

"You mentioned someone else," Paisley said.

"Rudy was concerned about a man named Cray," Carlita said. "He told Cool Bones he may have stepped on a toe or two and also commented about how bookies were a paranoid bunch. If we can find this Cray person…"

"I'm sure the cops are already working that angle," Paisley interrupted. "Although technically, it's Cool Bones' word against Culpepper's."

"It all goes back to incriminating evidence," Carlita said. "Mercedes might be onto something. What if McCoy's killer witnessed the two men arguing and saw an opportunity to take him out?"

Bang. Carlita turned to find a woman, plump and sporting shoulder length gray hair, standing in the doorway.

She squared her shoulders and made her way over. "Hello. We're looking for Eunice Culpepper."

"I'm Eunice Culpepper."

"I'm Carlita Taylor. I own an apartment building over in Walton Square. My neighbor." Carlita motioned to Paisley. "Mentioned the owner of this building might be interested in selling."

Culpepper squinted her eyes. "Paisley?"

"Hello, Mrs. Culpepper. We didn't mean to bother you. I thought I overheard you telling Steve you planned to sell this place. I mentioned it to Mrs. Taylor. We decided to come by and take a look around," Paisley fibbed.

"I don't recall mentioning it to Steve," the woman said. "Although I have been tossing around the idea of selling and finding a small condo on the water."

"The exterior of the property looks...promising," Carlita said. "I hate to impose, but wondered if it would be okay if we took a quick look around."

"You'll have to look past the clutter. I've been working on clearing it out." Culpepper warily eyed Rambo. "Does your dog bite?"

"He only nibbles," Mercedes joked.

The woman pressed her hand to her chest.

"I'm kidding. Rambo won't bite you."

"Pets aren't allowed in my building. He'll need to stay outside."

"I'll hang out with Rambo," Paisley offered.

Mother and daughter climbed the porch steps and entered a narrow hall. To the left was a door marked "1B." Farther down and on the other side of the hallway was a "1A."

"This is my unit. There are only four. Two main floor units and two upper units." Culpepper flung the door open and ushered them inside.

Paperback books, reaching all the way to the ceiling, filled an entire wall. Stacks of yellow newspapers lined the bay window. Empty chip bags, piles of blankets, pairs of slippers, discarded shirts and shoes, along with a stack of laundry baskets, cluttered the floor.

In between the clutter, a small path had been carved out, leading from the living room into the dining area.

Carlita, keeping one eye on where she walked, followed the woman into the kitchen. Filling the kitchen counters and table were stacks of pots and pans, plates, cups and bowls, boxes of cereal, loaves of bread, and canned goods. The sink overflowed with dirty dishes.

She could feel her stomach churn at the lingering stench...a combination of grease and rotten fruit.

A fly buzzed by and landed on a bowl of food covered in a thin layer of mold.

"Like I said, it's a little messy, but at least you can get an idea of the layout," Culpepper said.

"A little messy?" Mercedes whispered in her mother's ear. "This place needs a bottle of bleach or, better yet, a bulldozer."

"The units all have good bones but need updating. Do you have a ballpark figure of what you want to offer?"

"I…uh…would have to run some numbers."

Culpepper cleared her throat. She stuck her finger in Carlita's face. "Don't try to lowball me. I know how valuable rental properties are in this area."

"I'm not trying to lowball you, but let's be honest. This place needs a lot of work."

"A *lot* of work," Mercedes stressed.

Carlita tiptoed to the kitchen sink overlooking the backyard. Hot, humid air seeped in through the open window. She could see Rambo sniffing around the garage while Paisley kept a close eye on him.

If Cool Bones and Rudy McCoy had been standing in the backyard, the woman would have a clear and unobstructed view of them from her window. Carlita had no doubt Mrs. Culpepper witnessed them arguing, maybe even saw McCoy swing his bat at Cool Bones.

"This might be a little more than I'm able to take on right now."

The trio finished the tour of the two bedrooms and equally cluttered bathroom before traipsing back outside.

"Thank you for the tour. I'll give you my telephone number." Carlita jotted her cell phone number on a slip of paper and handed it to her. "If you decide you're serious about selling, call me."

"I will." The woman turned to Paisley. "Tell Steve hello for me and I'll see him soon for my next ink.

He's such a nice guy. He reminds me of someone I once knew in high school."

"Steve mentioned he was working on a complicated tattoo for you," Mercedes said. "I've seen some of his stuff. He does nice work."

"He's a top-tier artist, a master at his craft." Culpepper tugged at her blouse's neckline, revealing a patch of bare skin. Bright blue eyes stared back at them.

On closer inspection, Carlita noticed only half of the facial features were skeletal. The other half was a young man, with dark hair curling around the nape of his neck.

"This is my deceased husband, Ronaldo."

"What an interesting place for a tattoo," Carlita said diplomatically.

"I'm keeping him close to my heart."

"I hope it brings you comfort. Thank you again for showing us around." Carlita waited until they were off the property and out of earshot. "What do you think?"

"The place is a dump," Mercedes said bluntly. "I have never seen so much stuff in my life. I'm starting to feel claustrophobic just thinking about it."

"It's a mess. I think she's a hoarder. I noticed a newspaper from 1999."

"I'm a little surprised. Mrs. Culpepper always struck me as neat and tidy, even commenting about the tattoo shop's cleanliness," Paisley said.

"She seems to like Steve," Mercedes said.

"Between you and me, I think she has a crush on him. She's always inviting him over for drinks and comments about how he reminds her of someone she once knew." Paisley changed the subject. "Did you find anything out about the dead tenant?"

"I was able to confirm Culpepper would have had a bird's-eye view of the argument between Rudy

McCoy and Cool Bones," Carlita said. "She can see the entire backyard from her kitchen window."

"Which means she would be considered an eyewitness," Paisley said.

"I have no doubt she saw what happened. The guy swung his bat at Cool Bones. He grabbed it and shoved McCoy to the ground. Fast forward. A hotshot investigator reopens the case. Culpepper sees a story about it on television and calls him, telling the new cold case investigator what she saw. They exhume McCoy's body. With new DNA technology, they're able to match a print on his bat to Cool Bones and arrest him."

"At the risk of stating the obvious, there's no smoking gun," Mercedes pointed out. "Mrs. Culpepper didn't see Cool Bones kill him."

"True, but there's a lot of evidence pointing in his direction. The fact they argued only hours before the guy's death. His print. The eyewitness. A new investigator who wants to make a name for himself," Carlita said. "I've been thinking about what you overheard on the bus during your community service."

"Officer Kean's comment."

"Yeah." Carlita glanced at her watch. "If we get a move on, we might have enough daylight hours to find out if the comment he made is, in fact, true."

Chapter 18

"Are we sure we wanna do this?" Mercedes warily peered out the window as their car crept down the gravel drive, entering the Bonaventure Cemetery. "This place is spooky at dusk."

"I like spooky." Paisley rubbed her palms together. "Dusk equals ghost peeping at its best. If you see a little girl walking around, don't be alarmed."

"Little Gracie Watkins," Mercedes said. "I heard the story about how people have seen her downtown, near where the Pulaski Hotel used to be."

"Bonaventure is bigger than I remember." Carlita eased the car off to the side and shifted into park. "Since we're running out of daylight, I figured we should try to find Rudy McCoy's grave first."

"We'll be able to cover more ground if we split up," Paisley said.

"I was thinking the same thing," Mercedes said.

Carlita shut the engine off. The trio climbed out and she locked the car doors. "I'll take the far left quadrant. Mercedes can search the far right while Paisley checks out the middle."

"Got it." Mercedes gave them a thumbs up. "Stay safe and holler if you need help."

"Like this?" Paisley screamed at the top of her lungs.

Carlita winced. "That'll do the trick."

With a plan in place, she and Rambo headed left. Walking at a brisk clip, they searched every square inch for signs of disturbed dirt.

The sun had already set and the majestic live oaks, dripping with moss, cast eerie shadows across the gravestones.

Hoot. Hoot...hoot...hoot. Carlita instinctively stumbled back. A great horned owl, perched on a tree limb, peered down at them.

Woof. Rambo charged toward the tree, dragging Carlita and his leash along with him. She tripped on a tree root, flew forward, and landed hard on her hands and knees.

"Rambo!"

Completely oblivious to her fall, Rambo barked loudly, pawing at the tree, daring the owl to swoop down. The owl cocked his head, unfazed by the attention.

Mercedes and Paisley, noticing Carlita was down on the ground, ran over.

"Are you okay?"

"I think so." Carlita grasped her daughter's outstretched hand and pulled herself to her feet. "Rambo chased after an owl. Unfortunately, I was holding his leash and tripped on a tree root."

"It's dangerous after dark," Paisley said. "I almost fell myself."

"For safety's sake, I think it would be best if we drive the rest of the way around." Carlita limped back to their starting point.

As soon as everyone was inside the car, she eased onto the gravel road, driving slow enough so Mercedes and Paisley could look for signs of recent activity.

They reached the corner and turned right, entering a newer section of the cemetery.

"Hang on. I think I see something," Paisley said.

"I do too." Carlita left the car idling in the event they needed to make a quick getaway. The trio trekked over to the spot, only to find a temporary headstone bearing a woman's name. "This isn't it."

"I think we're wasting our time." Carlita turned to go.

"Wait. I see something over on this side." Mercedes turned her cell phone's flashlight on and shined it on the headstone: *Rudolph "Rudy" McCoy*. Below his headstone was a date, along with: *Friend and son, sorely missed.*

"I can't believe we actually found it." Carlita clasped her hands, solemnly reflecting on McCoy's final resting place. "May he continue to rest in peace."

"Not recently, he hasn't." Mercedes motioned to the fresh dirt and visible mound.

Carlita squinted her eyes, surveying the nearby plots for signs of graves recently dug up. "I'm not sure we're going to find anything else. We could be at this all night."

"At the risk of stating the obvious, this isn't the only cemetery in town," Paisley said. "For all we know, the cops could be focusing their investigation on another cemetery."

"Good point." Carlita returned to the car and waited for the women to climb in before driving off. "I say we call it a day."

"Or a night." Mercedes grew quiet, watching her mother crisscross through the cemetery. "Where are you going?"

"I have no idea. I think I got turned around." Making two more turns, Carlita passed by McCoy's gravesite. "We're going in circles."

"Turn left at the stop sign."

Carlita turned left, passing by a familiar landmark, one she'd noticed on the way in. "Thanks, Mercedes. I think we're heading the right way now."

A car crested a small hill. Bright headlights nearly blinded Carlita.

"The jerk has his brights on," Mercedes said.

A spotlight illuminated the entire interior of the car. "Whoa." Paisley squeezed her eyes shut. "I think my retinas just got burned."

Carlita tightened her grip on the steering wheel, watching as the vehicle made a sudden hard turn, blocking their only exit. "We're trapped."

Chapter 19

Mercedes blurted out the first thing that popped into her head. "We're going to be robbed."

"In a cemetery?" Paisley wrinkled her nose. "Robbed of what?"

"We aren't getting robbed." Carlita pointed out the bubble on top of the car. "It's the cops. What time does the cemetery close?"

"Do cemeteries close?"

The driver's side door opened. With a light hand on his holster, a uniformed officer approached Carlita's side of the car.

She rolled the window down. "Good evening."

"Hello, ma'am." He leaned in, shining his flashlight inside the car. "Can I ask you what you're doing?"

"Visiting a gravesite," Carlita said. "We didn't realize it was getting so late. We were trying to find our way out and got turned around. Is there a problem?"

"We received a report of suspicious activity."

"I can assure you we weren't doing anything suspicious," Mercedes said.

"Can I see some identification?"

Carlita fumbled around inside her wallet, removed her license, and handed it to him.

"I'll be back." The officer returned to his vehicle.

The minutes ticked by.

Carlita sucked in a breath. "What's taking him so long?"

"I don't want to get all up in your business, Mrs. T, but the officer isn't going to find anything when he runs a check on your license, is he?" Paisley asked.

"Not that I can recall. I mean, I'll be the first to admit we're no strangers to the Savannah police force, but I'm pretty sure my record is clean."

Another two…then three…followed by four minutes passed. Finally, the officer returned. He handed Carlita her license. "I would like to see the other occupants' licenses as well."

Paisley promptly handed her license to him. Mercedes was a little more reluctant to the point the cop commented about it. "You can't find your license?"

"It's…uh…in here somewhere." Mercedes held it out. "The picture is kinda dated, but it's me."

He turned his flashlight on the license before flashing it toward Mercedes. "Mercedes Garlucci. Why does your name ring a bell?"

"I had a minor confrontation with Officer Perkins a couple of days ago down at the Thirsty Crow."

"Ah." The cop cleared his throat. "You were the person who threw a beer bottle at Perkins."

"At the risk of appearing disrespectful, I can assure you I did not throw the bottle. For the record, there were no eyewitnesses to verify either."

He motioned to Paisley. "Anything you want to share about your identity before I run it through?"

"No. I'm clean." Paisley watched the officer return to his patrol car. "At least I hope so. I was pulled over a few weeks ago by a traffic cop but I don't think he took note of my name."

"We didn't do anything wrong," Mercedes insisted. "He'll check our IDs and let us leave."

Ting. Carlita grabbed her cell phone from the center console. "Pete's wondering where we are."

She tapped out a quick reply. *Mercedes, Paisley, and I swung by the cemetery. We'll be heading home soon.*

Pete: *Cemetery?*

Carlita: *To see if investigators dug up anyone other than Rudy McCoy.*

Pete: *The local cemeteries close at dusk.*

Carlita: *Now you tell me.*

"Here he comes," Paisley breathed.

The officer returned to the driver's side and handed their licenses back. "You're free to go. For future reference, the cemetery closes at dark."

"We didn't realize it was getting so late." Carlita apologized and promised him they were on the way out.

The cop headed back to his vehicle. He swung around in a circle and pulled off to the side, motioning for them to go ahead.

Carlita crept past, briefly wondering if it was too good to be true and they were off the hook. She checked for traffic before pulling onto the street.

Paisley glanced over her shoulder. "He's following us."

"Cool. We get a police escort home," Mercedes joked. "Must be a slow night."

"I have no intention of making it any more exciting."

They reached a major intersection and Carlita turned toward home.

"He went the other way," Paisley said.

Carlita reached Walton Square and stopped in front of *Shades of Ink*. "I'm sorry we took so long."

"Don't apologize. I'm glad I invited myself." Paisley scooted across the backseat and reached for the door handle. "In case you're interested, I asked Steve about Mrs. Culpepper's next tattoo appointment. It's tomorrow morning at ten. There he is now."

Steve exited his shop and stepped over to the car. "Paisley told me you got stopped by the cops over at the cemetery. Bonaventure has had a little trouble lately with people hanging out there after dark."

"All we wanted to do was look around to see if the cops were exhuming other bodies."

"Did you find anything?"

"Nope. I should've realized there are several cemeteries nearby. Figuring out if the investigators are following up on other leads would take days, maybe even weeks." Carlita sighed. "We could be chasing our tails."

Steve lit a cigarette. "How did it go over at Mrs. Culpepper's place?"

Carlita filled him in on what happened. "She seems to like you."

Paisley playfully nudged her boyfriend. "She has the hots for my man."

He nudged her back. "You have nothing to worry about. She'll be in tomorrow morning for her next round of ink."

Carlita drummed her fingers on the steering wheel. "Mrs. Culpepper is one of the reasons Cool Bones is behind bars. Her eyewitness testimony is why the cold case investigator started digging around."

"True," Mercedes agreed.

"Cool Bones didn't deny he and Rudy McCoy argued right before his death. Although he was still alive when Cool Bones left, his body was found in his apartment," Carlita said. "What if she saw more than she told authorities?"

"Meaning she only gave them a partial version of what happened that day?" Mercedes asked.

"Maybe she forgot some very important details and needs a little help jogging her memory."

Paisley rubbed her palms together. "And Steve might be the perfect person to help clear out the cobwebs."

He took a long drag off his cigarette and blew the smoke away from them. "You want me to see what I can find out?"

"If you don't mind," Carlita said. "Cool Bones needs all the help he can get."

"He's my friend too. I hate the thought of him being convicted of a crime he didn't commit. I have surveillance all over the place thanks to Elvira selling me her friends and family package a couple years ago," Steve joked. "Her every word can be recorded."

Carlita stared at him, a sudden idea popping into her head. "You gave me an idea."

"I know where you're going with this Ma." Mercedes tapped her phone's screen. "What time is Culpepper coming in?"

"I'm almost positive it's ten o'clock."

"Ravello's doesn't open until eleven," Carlita said. "Do you mind if I hang around in the back of the shop to listen in?"

"Not at all. A little forewarning. She's a stickler for punctuality and sometimes arrives a few minutes early."

"Thursday is my staff meeting at Ravello's," Carlita said. "I could postpone it."

"I can handle it for you, Ma."

"Yes, you can. I'm going to take you up on the offer." Carlita gave Steve a high five. "I'll see you tomorrow morning at quarter 'til ten."

Chapter 20

After dropping Paisley off, Carlita circled around the block to Mercedes' apartment.

She pulled into the alley and crept to the end, barely squeezing by the dumpster, which sat at an odd angle, almost blocking the lane. "Somebody moved the dumpster."

"Why would someone move the dumpster?" Mercedes hopped out.

Carlita unbuckled her seatbelt and caught up with her daughter in front of the metal bin.

Working together, the women slid the metal container back to its original spot. "She's already at it."

"Who is at what?" Mercedes asked.

"Elvira. Snitch is telling Elvira there's a tubby treasure."

"You think Snitch was spying on you, listening in and went back to Elvira to report what she heard?"

"I know for a fact." Carlita tapped the top of the metal bin. "If you hear any banging around, it will be Elvira dumpster diving."

"Why would she think the dumpster is a tub?"

"Who knows? All I know is the woman never gives up."

"Never."

Carlita gave her daughter a quick hug. "Thanks for handling the staff meeting for me tomorrow."

"You're welcome. Good luck."

"I'll let you know how it goes." Carlita waited until Mercedes was safely inside and her living room lights turned on before driving off.

Perhaps Mrs. Culpepper would remember something. Or maybe not. Either way, it was worth a try.

She briefly wondered how her friend and tenant was doing. As soon as she pulled into her parking spot at home, she logged onto the jail's website and scheduled a visit for the following day.

Hopefully, Cool Bones had taken the time to go over his bookie journal and would remember something, some small detail, to give them a much-needed break in the case.

Thinking Pete was still working at the restaurant, she made a beeline for his office and found it empty. Dropping her purse and Rambo off at home, she returned downstairs and stopped by the hostess station.

"Is Pete here?"

"Hey, Carlita. He left with a woman a few minutes ago." The hostess described Elvira.

"Does she talk like this?" Carlita imitated Elvira's whiny voice.

"Yes. That's her. Pete seemed somewhat aggravated. She kept saying something about a tub."

Carlita grinned. "Elvira."

"That was her name. Elvira."

"I bet they're out back." Carlita made a move toward the door.

The hostess stopped her. "Actually, I think they said something about a tunnel."

"Ah. Thanks." Carlita trekked through the main dining room to the stairs. As she neared the bottom, she discovered the door was unlocked. Picking up the pace, she strode along the tunnel corridor, turning when she reached the intersection leading to Parrot House's access point.

Faint voices echoed from within, growing louder with each step she took.

Carlita called out. No one answered, so she kept walking. As she drew closer to the excavation area, she heard Elvira's distinctive voice and Pete's muffled reply.

She climbed over the wall. "There you are. The hostess thought I might find you down here."

"Elvira and I were discussing the project's progress."

"More like non-progress," Elvira corrected. "I'm beginning to think these clowns are intentionally dragging their feet."

"We can't place all the blame on them," Pete said. "We're the ones who restricted their access, only allowing them in here when we're present."

"Poindexter should be here any minute." Elvira tapped the top of her watch. "We're going to put together a revised work schedule. Time is money."

"Don't even think about throwing your weight around," Pete warned. "You seem to have trouble remembering this is my property."

"And lest you forget, this is *our* project."

Carlita noted the frustration in her husband's eyes. Elvira was, once again, treading on thin ice. She stepped in between them and did a timeout. "Cooler heads need to prevail."

"You would think you would want to get this project moving."

"I am eager to see the disruption end. However, I have multiple businesses to run in the meantime."

"And I don't?" Elvira asked incredulously.

"We're all busy," Carlita said. "By the way, I dropped Mercedes off at home and found the dumpster blocking part of the alley."

Elvira's eyes slid to the side. "Someone moved the dumpster?"

"Maybe you can take a look at your surveillance cameras when you get home."

"Who would want to mess with a dumpster?"

"Someone who is searching for something. Maybe a tub?" Pete rubbed his chin, his expression flicking from aggravation to amusement. "Perhaps treasure?"

Elvira made a choking sound. "You! You told Snitch there was treasure."

Carlita patted her pockets. "I don't have my purse on me. I owe you ten bucks, Pete."

"You two placed a bet my bird was spying on you?" Elvira feigned indignation. "I'm offended."

"Offended by the truth?"

"I didn't intentionally have Snitch spy on you. However, she has been trained to listen in."

"And you thought why not take a look around." Pete sighed. "We were messing with Snitch. There isn't any treasure hidden in, around, or near a dumpster."

"Besides. A tubby is not a dumpster. Not even close."

Elvira stomped her foot. "I knew it! Snitch was talking about your old hot tub out back."

"Seriously." Carlita lifted her hand. "We were messing with Snitch."

"Are you sure?" She eyed them skeptically.

Carlita made an "x" across her chest. "Promise."

Arvid Poindexter, the local historian and archaeologist Pete had hired, appeared, ending their conversation. "I hate to interrupt what sounds like an intriguing discussion."

Pete motioned him inside. "Thank you for coming by. My...colleague...and I use the term colleague loosely, is concerned about the time it's taking to make progress on this project."

"Because of the limited access," Arvid said. "If my team had more hours available, we could move faster."

"I agree." Pete rubbed his palms together. "We need to pick up the pace."

Carlita, determined to stay out of it, let the trio hammer out a revised schedule, increasing the number of hours the workers were allowed on site.

While they chatted, she noticed Elvira slip away, cell phone in hand. She returned near the end of the conversation, working out the details of when she could be there to oversee the project.

The archaeologist was the first to leave, promising to be there the following day with his team.

Elvira and Carlita waited in the tunnel corridor while Pete turned the lights off. Reaching the first of a series of doors, he triple locked it. They continued walking. All the while, Elvira lamented about how they hadn't found anything significant.

"You can always call it quits," Pete suggested.

"Not on your life. I've come too far to give up now."

The trio returned to the main floor and gathered on the front porch.

"Where's your van?" Carlita asked.

"I walked here."

"I can give you a ride home." Pete jangled his keys.

"Thanks for the offer. I could use a little exercise and fresh air."

The couple exchanged a puzzled glance. Elvira and exercise were not two words often used in the same sentence.

"Suit yourself."

Elvira patted the backpack she was carrying and began whistling loudly as she strolled down the sidewalk, making her way toward the street.

Pete reached for Carlita's hand and held the door.

"Hang on." She stopped him. "When is the last time Elvira went on a casual stroll after dark by herself?"

"My guess would be never," Pete said. "You think she's up to something?"

"I have my suspicions. Let's hang out here for a couple of minutes."

A minute ticked by and then two. Carlita reached for the doorknob. "Let's go."

"Go where?"

"To see if my hunch is correct." She slipped out of the building, with Pete close behind.

He turned to go in the direction he'd seen Elvira heading.

Carlita stopped him. "This way." She grabbed his arm, tiptoeing past his truck.

Veering left, they crept alongside the recycling bins.

Ping. A shadowy figure flitted past.

The ping was followed by a muffled *crack*.

Immediately following the *crack* was a loud splash.

Chapter 21

Pete raced across the parking lot to their private patio in the back. Carlita caught up with him, coming to an abrupt halt at what they found.

Elvira, with legs straight up in the air, splashed around inside their old hot tub, full of moldy black water. Visible above the water line was a snorkel tube.

Droplets of the hot tub's slimy contents pelted Carlita's face. "Her foot is tangled in the trellis."

"How did she get tangled up in the trellis?" Pete stepped onto the tub's wooden deck. Grabbing hold of Elvira's arm, he lifted her up and out of the water.

"I'm stuck," she gasped.

"You got hung up on the trellis." On closer inspection, Carlita noticed her flip-flop was caught on a section of lattice.

"Hold still," Pete ordered.

The troublesome woman promptly stopped moving. "Hurry up. This water stinks. My gag reflex is kicking in and I'm feeling faint."

"We can only hope something shuts you up."

"And teaches you a lesson," Carlita added.

While Pete held Elvira's leg steady, Carlita snapped the rotting piece of wood in two and removed it from her ankle. "Your foot is free. Do you need a hand?"

"I wish I had a hand," Elvira panted. "I'm caught on something else."

Using his cell phone's flashlight, Pete shined it into the murky water. "I must say, you got yourself into a bind this time."

"Literally."

"What is it?" Carlita leaned over the edge, struggling to see.

"From what I can tell, her sleeve is caught on a broken jet. I'm going to have to climb in." Pete waded into the water.

"Can you hurry?" Elvira's voice grew faint. "Wooziness is settling in."

"I have half a mind to leave you here," Pete said.

"Only Elvira can get trapped in a hot tub."

Using both hands, Pete yanked on her sleeve.

Rip.

"You're free."

Elvira scrambled over the side. "This hot tub is a deathtrap."

"It was secured and covered last I checked. You should save your snorkeling endeavors for daylight hours," Carlita lectured. "If Pete and I hadn't come out here and found you, who knows how long you would have been stuck."

Elvira scraped a splotch of slimy mold from her chin. "Gross."

"Why were you in the hot tub?" Carlita folded her arms, pinning her former neighbor with a hard stare. "We told you there was nothing here."

"I know. Unfortunately, as I was crossing the parking lot, it caught my eye. I figured I would take a quick look inside. I tripped on the broken lattice. Next thing I know…" Elvira made a diving motion with her hand. "Bam! I'm in the water and upside down. It's a good thing I had the snorkel."

"I should've let you percolate in your predicament and called the police to report a trespasser," Pete said.

Elvira's jaw dropped. "You would not."

"If you ever pull that stunt again, I will."

Elvira mumbled something unintelligible under her breath.

"What did you say?"

"I said, 'thank you very much.' Ciao." Elvira power-walked across the parking lot, leaving a trail of water in her wake.

"Never a dull moment with her." Pete shook his head.

"Never." Carlita doubled over, bursting into fits of laughter. "It is kind of our fault. In her defense, it's not in her DNA to *not* look for treasure. The tub was too much of a temptation."

"I hope she learned her lesson."

Carlita popped onto the tips of her toes and kissed Pete's cheek. "Thank you for rescuing Elvira. I'm sure she'll think twice before she goes hot tub snorkeling after dark again."

*****

Carlita woke early the next morning. It had been a restless night spent tossing and turning, worrying about Cool Bones, and trying to figure out how they were going to prove his innocence.

A small niggling voice in the back of her mind wondered if he *had* committed the crime and murdered his competitor. Perhaps he'd done so in a moment of rage. She knew Cool Bones, but how well did she really know him?

She pushed the thought aside. He'd been nothing but an ideal tenant, a true friend. Calm and steady. Always on an even keel. In fact, Carlita couldn't remember ever seeing him lose his temper.

On the other hand, you never knew a person unless you lived under the same roof. Maybe not even then. Serial killers were an excellent example. She'd read stories about how family members had no idea their loved ones were killers.

There was still the big question mark about the mystery man. "Cray." If Carlita could find Cray, or at the very least figure out who he was, she might be on the trail to piecing together what happened that day at 2012 Gleason Street.

Carlita rolled over and found Pete was already out of bed. She caught him as he was heading out the door, on his way to the Flying Gunner to meet with his staff.

After he left, she poured herself a cup of coffee, grabbed a pen and began jotting notes:

- Who were the other tenants living in McCoy's building at the time of his death? (Culpepper)
- Names of other bookies Cool Bones might remember. Question him about the mysterious "Cray."

Logging onto the computer, she typed McCoy's name in the search bar, her heart plummeting when she found a story released the previous day about the cold case investigation. The author told readers Charles Benson, aka Cool Bones, a prominent local musician, had been charged with the murder.

Scrolling to the comment section, she was glad to discover the replies were all supportive of Cool Bones, some who even knew him personally.

She finished scrolling and read several older stories, but couldn't find anything that might be a clue.

Although it was still early, she grabbed her purse and made her way to Walton Square. With time to kill, she swung by the pawn shop.

Tony was in the back and seated at the desk. "Hey, Ma."

"Hey, Son." Carlita hugged him. "How's business?"

"A little slow. We've officially entered the summer slump."

"I'm sure things will pick up soon."

"I'm thinking about running an ad in the local paper." Tony handed her his iPad.

Carlita slid her reading glasses on and studied the screen. Front and center, in big bold letters, was the slogan, *Swap and Shop in Savannah*. The backdrop was a quaint, cozy store with a brick walkway. A pink and blue striped awning ran the length of the building. A tabby cat was curled up in the picture window.

"Catchy, huh?"

"I like it. I like the image. It evokes thoughts of small town coziness."

"Thanks. Shelby helped me find the picture. I figured it was worth a try to drum up some business."

"Good luck. I hope it works."

"Me too." Tony stood. "You heading to Ravello's?"

"Shades of Ink." Carlita told him about Mrs. Culpepper's tattoo appointment and her plan to eavesdrop. "Steve's gonna try to help."

"Duke was in here yesterday," Tony said. "He told me Cool Bones is down in the dumps."

"I made an appointment to go visit him at the jail after listening in on what Culpepper has to say." Carlita shifted her purse to her other arm. "I was wondering if I should call Shelby to see if she needs any help in getting ready for the baby's arrival."

"She's all set. The only thing we need now is more room. You oughta see the apartment."

"I saw it the other day when Mercedes and I took the baby gifts over after the shower. It's packed."

"Packed, cramped, stuffed. We're packed in like sardines. I never realized babies needed so much stuff."

"For such tiny humans, they require a lot of equipment," she joked. "I haven't given you and Shelby my gift for the baby."

"You don't have to Ma. You and Mercedes hosting the shower was enough."

"But there is something else. Is Shelby around?"

"Yeah. She and Violet are hanging out at home today."

Carlita twined her fingers. "This might work out perfectly. Can you see if she has time to meet us in the alley?"

"Sure." Tony made the quick call, relaying the message and asking his wife to meet him and his mother. "She and Violet are on the way."

With a quick word to his employee, he caught up with Carlita on the front sidewalk. Circling around, they joined Shelby and Violet, who stood waiting for them in the alley.

"I had hoped to have Pete and Mercedes here when I gave you your gift, but getting everyone together is next to impossible."

Using her key, Carlita opened the storage room door, a room she'd cleared out and cleaned out months earlier in anticipation of the new project. She flipped the lights on and stepped aside. "Welcome home."

Shelby stared in disbelief. "What is this?"

"More space," Carlita said. "For you."

Tony blinked rapidly, struggling to take it all in. "It looks like a brand new apartment."

"Almost." Carlita beamed, proud of what she and Bob Lowman had accomplished in a short amount of time. Working almost around the clock, he and his construction crew had transformed the space, creating three bedrooms and two full bathrooms with flex space to boot.

Some minor finishes were still needed—adding trim boards and installing ceiling fans and bathroom mirrors. The last step was connecting the new interior staircase to the upper level, a project Bob assured Carlita could be done with minimal disruption to the family.

"Nana has a new house," Violet announced.

"*You* have a new house," Carlita corrected. "At least a partial addition. Go ahead. Look around."

With tears in her eyes, Shelby grasped Violet's hand. While the small family explored, Carlita stood near the door, watching them make their way from room to room.

Tony followed his wife and daughter back to the entrance. "How did you get this done so fast?"

"With a lot of careful planning, making sure I scheduled the construction well in advance."

"No wonder you were pushing so hard for us to take a long vacation away from home." Tony wagged his finger at his mother. "You had this planned all along."

"Guilty as charged." Carlita pointed to the stairs. "As you can see, the stairs are ready to go. As soon as the interior stairwell is connected, Bob will remove the alley stairs, making it a seamless transition."

"We can fill this up, no problem," Tony said.

"He had a good idea, if you're interested." She shared his suggestion, to tear out the wall between the existing living room and main bedroom, giving them additional family space on the upper level.

"He already has it in his schedule and can complete it within a day or so."

"Tomorrow?" Shelby asked. "Would tomorrow be too soon?"

"As soon as you're ready."

Violet flung her arms around Carlita. "This is the best baby present ever."

"It's a family gift for all of you...from Pete, me and Mercedes."

"This must've cost an arm and a leg," Tony said. "We have some cash set aside. Shelby and I can reimburse you for the cost."

Carlita shook her head. "I still had our cut of the Marshland Isles' diamond money and figured this was the perfect way to put the money to good use."

"Are you sure?"

"Positive. I can't think of a single solitary thing I would rather spend it on."

Tony, with tears in his eyes, hugged his mother. "Have I ever told you that you're the best mother a son could ask for?"

A slow smile spread across Carlita's face. "And I have the best bunch of kids and daughters-in-law on the planet, not to mention grandkids."

"I better get back to work."

Shelby hugged Carlita. "Thank you," she whispered. "This is the best gift ever."

"You're welcome. I hope you live here for many years, making forever memories."

"We will. I can promise you we will."

Carlita watched her son and his family make their way to the alley. Tony's steps were lighter and his back straighter, as if a huge weight had been lifted off his shoulders. God had blessed her growing family beyond measure.

She trailed behind her family, heading to the *Shades of Ink* tattoo shop. It was time to find out if Eunice Culpepper could help. Leads were drying up and Carlita was growing concerned.

Chapter 22

"Where should I hide?" Carlita stood just inside the door of Steve Winter's tattoo shop and looked around. A cashier's counter and compact waiting area, complete with end tables and ink magazines, were off to the right.

To the left was a trio of massage tables, padded chairs and work carts. A straight shot and in the back was a hallway, a restroom, and a storage closet. Beyond that was a set of stairs leading to a second-story apartment.

"I was thinking in the dressing room." Steve motioned Carlita to follow him around the tables, to a narrow hall she'd never noticed before. On the other side were square cubicles sporting red curtains instead of doors.

"You have dressing rooms?"

"Some of my client's requested artwork is for more...remote body parts, which means gowns are required so I can access the skin."

Carlita wrinkled her nose. "I was gonna ask but on second thought, I'll leave it to my imagination."

"A wise decision." Steve patted the bench seat. "I'll put Culpepper as close as possible so you can listen in."

"Thanks, Steve. I appreciate it."

"And all you want me to do is find out what this woman knows about Rudy McCoy's death."

"Correct. We're missing something. Maybe ask her who her other tenants were. Someone else was lurking around the apartment building the day he was murdered. She may have a repressed memory that still needs to surface."

"Kind of like her remembering she'd seen Cool Bones."

"Exactly. At least that's what I'm hoping. Cool Bones mentioned the name Cray and even wrote it down in his bookie journal. You could throw it out there and see if you get a bite."

"I'll do my best," he promised. "I've given it some thought and already know how I'll bring the subject up. I'll mention Paisley and you stopping by and go from there."

"Sounds like you don't need my help." Carlita slid the curtain aside. "How long will it take to add her new layer of ink?"

Steve did a rough calculation. "Should be under an hour."

"The reason I'm asking is I scheduled an appointment to visit Cool Bones at eleven thirty."

"No problem. You'll be out in plenty of time."

"Great." Carlita pulled the curtain shut and eased onto the bench.

At exactly ten on the dot, she heard Steve's voice and another higher pitched voice. Carlita slid off the seat and peeked out, watching Steve escort Eunice Culpepper to a massage table. "...didn't want to be late. I had an unexpected errand to run."

"You're right on time."

She set her purse on the chair before climbing onto the table. "How many more sessions will I need before we finish my new tat?"

"I figure one more after this. We're almost done."

"Bummer. I've been enjoying our conversations."

"You have plenty of open spots left to cover," Steve joked. "Lean back, place your arm on the table, and we'll get started."

"I'm thinking about it...another tattoo, I mean." Culpepper let out a faint groan, resting flat, her arm extended.

Through the gap in the curtain, Carlita watched Steve wheel his cart closer. He rummaged around in the drawers, removing tools and placing them on top.

"Paisley mentioned you might be interested in selling your apartment building. Our friend Carlita Taylor is thinking about buying it."

"I'm not sure. I've lived there for so long now. I have no idea where I would go."

Rattling ensued, followed by the hum of equipment.

"What area of town are you in?"

Carlita averted her gaze when Steve pressed the tattoo gun against the woman's skin.

"Over on Gleason Street. Do you know where that is?"

"Gleason Street." Steve repeated the name. "Why does it sound familiar?"

"Because it was in the news." Culpepper had inadvertently given him the perfect opening to question her about Rudy McCoy's death.

"You're right. Something about the murder of a minor league baseball player."

"My tenant," she said.

"No kidding. You were the person who saw what happened?"

"I saw the killer and Rudy argue in the backyard. Hours later, my tenant was dead. The cause of death was blunt force trauma." Culpepper told him the story, similar to what Cool Bones had shared with Carlita and Mercedes, how she'd witnessed them arguing.

"Rudy took a swing at Charles Benson. I believe he also goes by the name Cool Bones. He grabbed the bat, knocked him to the ground and yelled at him."

"Do you know what he said?"

"I sure do. He said, 'I'm gonna finish you and you can bet on that.'"

"And then he killed him?"

"No. My guess is he came back later." Culpepper suggested Cool Bones knew he was being watched. "He knew I was there. He left and later sneaked back over."

"Did you speak with your tenant after you caught the two men arguing?" Steve asked.

"Yep. He said he was afraid of Cray. I took it to be Mr. Benson's nickname."

"You said he goes by Cool Bones."

"You know those bookies. They use various aliases," Culpepper said. "One day he's Cool Bones. The next he's Cray."

"Who found Mr. McCoy's body?"

"The police. A relative was trying to reach him. They requested a wellness check. The cops showed up on my doorstep, asking for access when no one answered his door."

"So...you let them into your tenant's apartment and that's when they found him?"

"Correct."

Steve leaned back in his chair. "We'll take a quick break before we move onto the next section."

Culpepper lowered her gaze, inspecting the new ink. "It looks great, even better than I envisioned. You do the best work. Topnotch. I recommend you to everyone I know."

"Thank you. I appreciate the referrals." Steve switched inks and guns and began working again. "I was thinking about what you said, how Mr. Benson came back to finish what he started. Blunt force trauma sounds messy."

"I'm sure, although I wasn't allowed in the apartment after it happened. It took a couple of days before the investigators let me back in. It's probably a good thing. A scene like that would have given me nightmares."

"What about the other tenants in the building?"

"The police questioned all of them. One of my tenants got so freaked out they moved," Culpepper said.

"I'll admit, I'm curious. You didn't hear yelling, screaming or any indication of an argument?" Steve asked.

"The investigators questioned me about it as well."

"And?" he prompted.

"I started giving it some serious thought. You see...I didn't remember much about what happened until recently. My memory has always been iffy, although it's improved recently due to me figuring out I have a vitamin deficiency."

"A vitamin deficiency?"

"B12, to be exact. B12 has helped improve my memory," Culpepper said. "I remembered something else, which is why I was almost late. I stopped by the police department to let the investigators know."

"Maybe I need some vitamin B12," Steve said.

"It's working miracles, at least for me."

"At the risk of me not minding my own business, what new detail did you remember?"

"I heard voices, men's voices. They were arguing. Rudy and another man."

"Did you see who it was?"

"Nope, and I don't recall the time either, although I know it was early evening."

Bam.

A metal sound similar to an object hitting the floor echoed.

"I am so sorry," Culpepper apologized. "I didn't mean to jerk my leg."

"Gotta be careful not to make sudden moves. You could get an extra ink design you didn't bargain for," Steve warned.

"I remember something else...just now, something about Rudy's death."

Carlita braced for what was coming next, hoping they would finally get their first big break in the case.

Chapter 23

"There was a black four-door sedan hanging around. I even asked Rudy about it," Mrs. Culpepper said.

"A black sedan," Steve repeated. "What did your tenant say?"

"I was being paranoid. I know what I saw. This vehicle was hanging around." Culpepper said something else, but it was too muffled for Carlita to hear.

"I hate to be the bearer of bad news, but black sedans are pretty common."

"Not this one. It had a red stripe along the side," she said. "There was a star symbol in the center of the stripe. So odd..."

As quietly as possible, Carlita tapped out a text to herself, a reminder to ask Cool Bones about a black sedan with a red stripe and star.

"I need to come by here more often," Culpepper said. "I'm remembering all kinds of stuff."

"Maybe pain jogs your memory," Steve kidded. "We're almost done."

The conversation shifted to the weather, summer, and her next appointment.

Another ten minutes passed. Carlita heard the bell jingle and the front door closed.

Steve appeared. "Did you catch all she said?" he asked.

"Most of it. She remembers hearing male voices and something about a black sedan hanging around."

"With a red stripe and star," Steve said. "I'm not sure how much it will help."

"A lot. Hopefully, it wasn't Cool Bones' black sedan." Carlita dusted her hands. "You're good at covert interrogations."

"Not bad for my first attempt, if I say so myself." Steve blew on his fisted hand and rubbed it against his shirt. "You said you were visiting Cool Bones today?"

"This morning. In fact, I should get going."

"Tell him to hang in there and keep the faith."

"I will." Carlita thanked him for letting her listen in and made the fast trek to the jail. Discovering she was early, she took a seat in the lobby to wait.

Visitors came and went. Men. Women. Old. Young. Children. A collection of humanity passed through the doors. Carlita thought about those who weren't fortunate enough to have visitors. Prisoners who had no one. No hope. Not a soul who cared, and it hurt her heart.

At least Cool Bones knew people cared and were trying to help.

"Carlita Taylor." She sprang from her seat and followed the guard down the long hall to a room close to the place she and Mercedes had previously visited him in.

Cool Bones was already there. He cast a somber look in her direction. His eyes were hollow. His demeanor reflected utter defeat. He slouched down in the chair as if sitting up straight was too much of an effort. "Hello, Carlita."

"Hello, Cool Bones." Carlita set her purse on the counter. "How are you holding up?"

"I gotta be honest. It's rough."

"I can only imagine."

He lowered his head. "I finally called Jordan to let her know what was going on."

Cool Bones' daughter, Jordan, and young granddaughter lived in Atlanta. Speaking about his loved ones always brought a smile to his face. Not today.

"How did she take it?"

"Okay." He shrugged. "She offered to come visit. I told her to wait until…" His voice trailed off.

"Until we could clear your name?"

"Or the judge locks me up for good."

"Listen, I know this looks bad."

"Bad?" Cool Bones laughed bitterly. "My public defender has already written me off. I'm as good as convicted."

"Then you need a new public defender."

"Why bother?"

"Because you're innocent. Before I forget, have you had a chance to look at your bookie journal?"

"Yeah. I don't remember most of my contacts."

"So…no clues…you found nothing significant or helpful?"

"I wish I had better news. The fact of the matter is, it was so long ago. Sure, I remember a few of the people. I could give you their names, but I think you would be chasing your tail. Unless you can pull a rabbit out of your hat, I'm doomed."

"What if I told you I had a rabbit and we're making some headway?"

For the first time since Carlita's arrival, a glimmer of hope flickered across his face. "You mean you have something?"

"Steve Winters gleaned new information not more than an hour ago. Mrs. Culpepper, who is one of his customers, remembers hearing men arguing after you left and before McCoy's death."

"It wasn't me. I left and never went back."

"We need to find out who it was. She mentioned the name Cray."

"Like I told you before, I don't remember anyone named Cray."

"But you wrote about him in your journal."

"I saw it. I've been racking my brain trying to figure out who it was, but still can't."

"According to Culpepper, she noticed a black sedan hanging around. It had a red stripe with some sort of star."

Cool Bones' brows furrowed. "The Brick District's clubhouse. I remember it now. The drivers drove black sedans with some sort of stripe and emblem on the side."

Carlita began scribbling in her notepad.

"I can tell you one thing. It wasn't me driving the fancy chauffeured vehicles. I had a beat-up VW van. Tangerine orange with a loud muffler," Cool Bones said.

"Did any of your bookie contacts drive a sedan with a red stripe, maybe even work for the Brick District's country club?"

He thought about it. "It's possible."

"This could be our most important clue." Carlita sprang from her chair and started to pace. Someone somewhere knew Cray or knew who drove a black sedan with a red stripe. "How many bookies were in the business back in the day?"

"If I had to guess, maybe a dozen in Savannah proper."

"A dozen bookies. All men?"

"Yeah. It wasn't a career most women would attempt then or even now," Cool Bones said. "I wasn't a part of their clique. They all kinda hung out in the same area."

Carlita abruptly stopped. "All the bookies back in the day hung out in the same place?"

"Yeah. Territory was important. So were contacts and connections. The Brick District was the place to be, where all the rich folks live, folks who had...have...money to burn."

"I've heard of it. It's the enclave to rival all enclaves," Carlita said. "It wouldn't hurt to do a little digging around."

"Good luck getting past the guard shack."

"If there's a will, there's a way." Carlita rubbed her brow. "I have the perfect person to ask. Someone who might be able to help."

The hall bell chimed, warning them their visit was coming to an end. Carlita gathered up her notepad and pen. "Keep the faith, Cool Bones. I'm going to find out who hung around the neighborhood and drove a black sedan with a red stripe and star if it's the last thing I do."

Chapter 24

Carlita exited the jail and climbed into her car before placing a call to her friend Tori Montgomery, a woman who hobnobbed with Savannah's upper echelon, a member of the elite society clubs, a person who could open doors no one else could.

Tori answered right away. "Hello, Carlita. I was just thinking about you and how much I enjoyed attending Shelby's baby shower."

"I'm glad you could make it. My only regret is we didn't have a lot of time to chat. It was hectic."

"Hectic, but in a good way. I planned to ask you about your tenant, Cool Bones. I heard he's gotten into a pinch of trouble," Tori said.

"More than a pinch. He's in jail, accused of murder."

"Charles Benson volunteered for a recent fundraiser to help raise money for the animal rescue center on Tybee Island." Tori told her she had a call into Mayor Puckett, a personal friend, inquiring about Cool Bones' release.

"I'm sure he would be thrilled. He needs all the help he can get." Carlita briefly filled her in, wrapping it up with how Mrs. Culpepper recalled seeing a black sedan with a red stripe lurking around the neighborhood. "Cool Bones thinks the Brick District's country club drivers drove similar sedans."

"They did and still do," Tori confirmed. "You remember Lucien."

"Of course I know Lucien, your driver and bodyguard."

"He once worked for the country club. Let me guess...you would like to go by there to do a little digging around."

"I only called to get information, but now that you mention it, doing a little digging around would be awesome."

Tori's voice grew muffled. "I haven't had lunch yet. If you're able, I can have Lucien chauffeur us over there."

"I hate to bother you on such short notice," Carlita said.

"It's no bother. While we're at it, we can catch up." Tori promised she and her driver would be there within half an hour.

"I don't know what to say, other than I owe you one."

"Nonsense. I'm never too busy to help a friend. See you soon."

The call ended, and Carlita drove straight home. She rummaged around in her closet, searching for country club attire before settling on a black skirt and pink silk blouse. She slipped a pair of black pumps on and critiqued her reflection in the mirror. "This'll have to do."

Grabbing a handbag, she ran downstairs to wait.

Tori's pale gray limousine pulled in only moments later. Lucien, her bodyguard and occasional driver, exited the vehicle and made his way around to her side.

"Hello, Lucien."

"Hello, Carlita. It's good to see you again."

"Same here."

He held the door and waited for her to slide in the back.

Tori sat on the opposite side, a welcoming smile on her face. "I meant to tell you the other day you're looking rested and content. Married life suits you."

"It does. Pete's a doll. Although I have to admit, it's been busy, busy."

"Ravello's is doing well?" Tori asked. "I confess I love watching Autumn's Divine Eats in Savannah

269

show, which regularly features your delightful Italian restaurant."

"You should stop by for dinner sometime. We would love to have you."

"I will," her friend promised.

While they rode, the women caught up. Tori was a friend you could go months without talking to, yet the moment you saw each other, the friendship and conversation picked up right where it left off.

The trip flew by, and before Carlita knew it, they were passing through massive wrought-iron gates, cruising along a city street with towering live oaks canopying over, creating a majestic tunnel of trees.

Meticulously manicured grounds lined both sides of the street. Bountiful gardens of vibrant flowers, in shades of pink, blue, yellow and crimson, swooped and dipped, creating a lush landscape for as far as the eye could see.

Carlita let out a low whistle. "The Brick District is decked out to the nines."

"It's the epitome of old money. Stately Savannah charm, where the who's who of the town live in mega mansions hand-crafted by artisans featuring imported finishes and furnishings sourced from all over the world," Tori said.

Carlita tilted her head, eyeing her friend with interest. "You make it sound like the most luxurious place on the planet, which makes me wonder why you don't live here."

"And leave Montgomery Hall to live a pretentious, ostentatious, snobbish existence?" Tori waved dismissively. "Not on your life. I'll take my quiet country manor any day."

"So...how did you get us in here, if you don't mind me asking."

"I have a lifetime membership." Tori rubbed her fingers and thumb together. "Money is money. Old money is even more desirable, at least in the eyes of the Brick District's members."

"I hope my outfit is up to snuff." Carlita smoothed her collar.

"You look fine. No one will give you a second glance."

The street wound past antebellum mansions, pillared palaces, and sprawling compounds, all gated and surrounded by thick brick walls. More majestic oaks dotted the yards.

Between the walls and gates, Carlita glimpsed circular driveways with hundreds of thousands of dollars' worth of vehicles parked out front. Maseratis. Lamborghinis. Even a few Porsche models. "I can't afford the air in this place," she joked.

"Like I said, this isn't my cup of tea," Tori said. "You couldn't pay me to live in the Brick District."

Carlita leaned forward and tapped Lucien's shoulder. "Tori mentioned you were once a Brick District driver."

"I was. Some of my friends still work here," Lucien said.

"Does the name Cray ring a bell?"

He repeated it. "No. I wasn't employed by them for long before Ms. Tori and I met, and she presented me with an offer I couldn't refuse. It was the best decision I ever made."

"And I can't envision not having you as a part of my family," Tori said fondly.

"What's the procedure for getting a job?" Carlita asked.

Lucien explained how he'd been referred by a friend of a friend. "You have to know somebody to get an interview. They also require background checks."

"They won't hire you if you have a record?"

Lucien laughed. "Not necessarily. Some have…shall we say…questionable hobbies."

Carlita's scalp tingled. "Questionable hobbies?"

"Betting is big in the Brick District. Horse betting, sports bets, you name it. Half the drivers I knew were bookies, and many still are." Lucien circled around, stopping beneath a pillared portico. Long, wide steps led to a massive porch. He escorted Tori from the limo first and then came around to Carlita's side.

Up the carpeted steps they climbed, stopping when they reached the reception desk. "Good afternoon, Ms. Montgomery."

Tori greeted the uniformed clubhouse employee by name. "Good afternoon, Darrel," she replied. "I didn't make a lunch reservation, but was hoping you could squeeze me and my friend in."

"Of course. We always have a spot for you. Would you care for dining room or patio seating?"

"First available will be fine. Near the window overlooking the portico would be preferable."

"Overlooking the portico?" Darrel lifted an eyebrow.

"My friend is hoping to see a Brick District sedan." Tori shifted her purse to her other arm. "Correct me if I'm wrong, but there is a stable of district drivers on the property."

"Close to forty at last count. I was once a district driver before transferring to the clubhouse."

"As was Lucien. I'm sure you've met."

"Lucien. Yes, ma'am. He's a good guy."

Carlita's heart skipped a beat. "I...uh...know someone who is interested in becoming a driver. If you don't mind me asking, how do you go about getting your foot in the door?"

Darrel pulled a notepad from behind the desk and jotted something down. He tore the paper off and handed it to Carlita. "If you have time, feel free to swing by the driver's office to chat with the supervisor on duty."

Tori patted his arm. "You've been most helpful, Darrel. Thank you."

The hostess arrived, menus in hand, and escorted them to their table near the front window. Their server appeared moments later. She delivered glasses of ice water and rattled off the daily special. "Our special today is roulade of oak smoked salmon salad with dill dressing."

Carlita carefully placed her menu on the table. "Salmon salad sounds perfect to me."

"I'll have the apple and butternut squash salad with the divine warm bread, along with crocks of your imported bordier churned butter." Tori ordered enough bread for two, insisting that once Carlita tasted it, she would want more.

"I know I already thanked you, but want you to know how much I appreciate you bringing me here to get a lay of the land."

"I'm thrilled I can assist in such a worthy cause," Tori said. "If you're not in a rush, we'll head to the driver's center when we're done. Do you have any idea who we might be looking for?"

"The man I mentioned earlier. Cray." Carlita tracked down the photos she'd taken of Cool Bones' bookie journal on her cell phone. "The deceased, Rudy McCoy, and Mrs. Culpepper both mentioned him."

Tori daintily sipped her water. "You don't have his given name?"

"Unfortunately, no." Carlita zoomed in on Cool Bones' journal entry and the man's name. "I know it's a longshot, but maybe we'll be able to figure out if this Cray person was a Brick District driver and if he's still around."

Lunch arrived fast and fresh. While they dined, Carlita told Tori about renovating her vacant storage area and surprising Tony and Shelby.

"I bet they're over the moon."

"Over the moon and in desperate need of more room," Carlita quipped. "The project will be finished in a matter of days, ready just in time for their growing family."

Tori nibbled on a shred of lettuce. "Do you miss the old neighborhood?"

"Walton Square?"

Her friend nodded.

"I suppose I would if not for the fact I'm over there almost every day. I think Mercedes is enjoying a little freedom and having the apartment all to herself."

"And Elvira?"

"Do I miss Elvira? No. She's always lurking somewhere nearby."

Tori laughed out loud. "I'm sure she is."

Carlita shared the story about Mercedes' and Elvira's arrests. "The judge fined them and ordered community service, picking up trash downtown."

"I bet Elvira was fit to be tied."

"Actually, I think Mercedes was more upset than Elvira. More like mortified when Sam showed up with a tour group."

"Oh, dear. Somehow, I don't envision your daughter being thrilled by having an audience."

"Not at all. Thank goodness Sam quickly saw the error of his ways. He apologized with the biggest bouquet of red roses I've ever seen and made plans for a romantic trip to Hilton Head."

"Sam Ivey is no dummy." Tori changed the subject. "You must bring Violet by sometime soon. Byron has mentioned her several times, how he misses having her around."

Tori's butler, Byron, had grown fond of Carlita's granddaughter. She reminded him of his granddaughter Lilly, who was struck and killed by a car on Bay Street a few years back. "I'll steal her away after the baby comes. We'll plan a visit and a day of fun for her."

"You're a wonderful mother and grandmother, Carlita. Pete's lucky to have you."

"We're lucky to have each other."

The meal ended, and Tori insisted on buying. Lucien, alerted by the staff the women were finishing, stood waiting in the pickup area.

"I trust you had an enjoyable lunch," he said as he escorted them to the limo.

"It was lovely. I feel richer already," Carlita joked.

"We would like to stop by the Brick District's driver's center," Tori said.

"To see if you can figure out who Cray is or was," Lucien guessed.

"Correct."

"I talked to a buddy who retired a few weeks ago. They still keep all their records."

"Of current and previous employees?" Carlita asked.

"Yes. I'm not sure how or where, but I know they keep them." Lucien hurried to the driver's side and climbed in. "My buddy, Scotty, seems to think if you grease the manager's palm, you might be able to get a little extra information."

"I'm game to try anything." Carlita clicked on the journal entry, double checking the date of McCoy's murder and Cool Bones' entry listing Cray's name. "It would be worth every penny."

Lucien turned onto the main thoroughfare, cruising past more mega mansions. They reached a roundabout and took the first turn to the right.

"This place is huge," Carlita said.

"Like its own small city," Tori said. "There are shops, restaurants, you name it. You could live in the Brick District and never have to leave."

A golfcart whizzed past, closely followed by another.

"All you need is a golf cart to get around," Carlita said.

"Along with bags of cash and massive connections," Tori added.

"The driver's center office is straight ahead." Lucien eased the car into an empty spot and climbed out. "Would you like me to escort you inside?"

"It won't be necessary," Tori said. "We shouldn't be long."

"We'll either figure out who Cray is or be back to square one," Carlita said. "Hopefully it's the former and not the latter."

Chapter 25

The nondescript fabricated metal building gave no hint about the interior of the Brick District's driver's center. In contrast to the exterior, it offered an upscale, modern feel.

A cluster of cubicles filled the center, while an array of offices lined the outer wall. Beyond the reception area was a wide open space. A display of exotic, expensive, and impressive cars filled the cavernous room. There was a little of everything—from sports cars to SUVs to limousines.

A woman wearing a crisp navy jacket and seated behind the desk greeted them. "Hello."

"Hello." Tori approached the counter. "Darrel at the clubhouse suggested we stop by. We're hoping to speak with the manager on duty."

"Are you needing information on renting a car?"

"No. We're hoping to inquire about a past or possibly current employee."

The woman cleared her throat, a look of concern on her face. "Was there a problem with one of our drivers?"

"Not a problem," Tori said. "We would, however, like to take it up with the person in charge."

"I'll need your name and address to log you into the system."

Tori gave her the information.

The woman's fingers flew over the computer keys. "You're not a Brick District resident."

"I am not. I live on Tybee Island," she said. "However, I am a lifetime club member."

The printer behind the receptionist made a whirring sound and spit out a single sheet of paper. "I've logged your request. Please wait here. I'll be right back."

Carlita watched her hurry off. "I think she was checking your credentials," she teased. "We might not get any info."

"We will. Once the manager finds out who I am," Tori assured her.

The woman returned, walking at a brisk pace. A man, stocky and wearing thick black glasses, followed close behind.

"Mrs. Montgomery?"

"I'm Victoria Montgomery," Tori said.

"It's my pleasure to meet you. I'm Jim Foster, the center's manager." The man grasped her hand, shaking it so hard her head wobbled. "I knew your husband, William. He was an incredible businessman and entrepreneur."

"He was," Tori agreed.

"What can I help you with today?"

"My friend is trying to track down a current or former employee. His name is Cray."

"Cray?" The manager shook his head. "We don't have anyone here by that name."

"Perhaps a previous employee," Carlita suggested. "We were told you keep records of all past and present employees."

"We do. Unfortunately, I'm not able to share personal information."

"Surely, you can take a quick look," Tori said.

"I'm sorry, Mrs. Montgomery," Foster apologized. "It's against company policy."

Carlita opened her purse. "Will a little persuasion in the way of cash sway you to bend the rules this once?"

"Don't bother. I'm not willing to risk my job for a favor or cash." Foster's expression grew grim. "If there's nothing else you need, perhaps you should leave."

"Very well." Tori clasped her hands. "An employee with integrity is hard to come by these days. I commend you for sticking to your guns."

The women turned to go.

Foster stopped them. "Good luck on your search. I hate for you to leave empty-handed. For the record, the Brick District's files are kept online."

"I see." Tori thanked him. With head held high, she strolled out of the office. She didn't slow until she and Carlita were back inside her limo.

Lucien waited for them to buckle up. "Someone named Puckett left a message with Montgomery Hall's housekeeper. He's been trying to reach you."

"Mayor Puckett?" Tori opened her purse and reached for her phone. "It appears I missed his call."

"He mentioned having an important update."

"It must be about Cool Bones." Tori promptly dialed the mayor's office. After the second transfer, she was finally connected.

Carlita quietly listened to the pleasantries, waiting for her friend to get to the point. "I'm hoping you have good news about the release of an old acquaintance, Charles Benson, a local musician."

Tori nodded her head. "Wonderful. Thank you, Clarence. I knew I could count on you." She ended the call and triumphantly waved her phone in the air. "Cool Bones will be free by the end of today."

"Did the mayor say how much his bond will be?" Carlita asked.

"Clarence pulled some strings. The judge ordered a minimal bond amount."

"This is the best news I've had since Cool Bones' arrest." Carlita whooped loudly. "I was thinking about what the manager said. He made a point of mentioning the drivers' records were online. It has me wondering."

"Wondering how you can crack into their system?"

"Yep," Carlita said. "And I know the perfect person to ask."

Chapter 26

At Carlita's request, Lucien dropped her off behind Ravello's. She spied Bob Lowman's work truck and wandered over to Shelby and Tony's new addition.

The *rat-a-tat-tat* of a nail gun filled the air, mingled with the echo of loud voices. She followed them to a secondary bedroom in the back where Bob and a trio of workers were installing trim boards.

Carlita hovered in the doorway until he noticed her. He gave a friendly wave and crossed the room. "Thank you for the heads up about Tony and Shelby learning about their new accommodations so me and my guys could finish without spoiling the surprise."

"I appreciate you playing along until I was able to share the exciting news," Carlita said. "And not a moment too soon. Shelby is due to have the baby any day now."

"I'm glad you're here. I have something to show you." Bob escorted her back outside, to the exterior of the building, where he told her his crew would start tearing out the old staircase. "We'll have this project wrapped up by the end of the week."

"Wonderful. The family is thrilled."

"Tony already stopped by to thank me," Bob said. "He told me they're interested in knocking down the upstairs wall you and I talked about."

"As you know, they're in desperate need of more room and now that they have extra bedrooms, it makes sense to expand the living room." Carlita chatted with Bob for a few more minutes, thanking him again for all of his hard work before crossing the alley.

Veering right, she walked to the end of the block and made another right, continuing until she reached EC Investigative Services front door. Elvira was seated at the desk. Dernice, who was also there, sat directly across from her.

"Spy," Snitch squawked.

"Carlita to you," Carlita joked.

"Carlita spy," the bird said. "Tubby treasure."

"Knock it off, Snitch. There is no tubby treasure."

"At least not in our hot tub." Carlita grinned.

"The bird is giving me a headache," Elvira grumbled.

"Maybe the headache is from getting stuck last night."

Dernice's head shot up. "What happened?"

"Elvira got caught on a lattice panel and ended up headfirst in our old hot tub. It's a good thing Pete and I found her when we did."

"That hunk of junk is a deathtrap," Elvira said. "I'm lucky I didn't drown."

"Yes, you are." Carlita sobered. "Pete emptied it. I'm sorry about your headache."

"It's okay. To be honest, you're right. It's my fault. You told me there was no treasure and yet I had to find out for myself." Elvira leaned back in her chair. "I see Lowman is next door finishing the reno project. I ran into Shelby. She's super excited."

"I wish everyone could have seen the looks on their faces when I took them over there."

"Not only did you do a good deed but think about the resale value if you ever decide to sell your slice of Savannah paradise," Dernice said.

"Hopefully it will be in the family for a long time, long after I'm dead and gone," Carlita said.

Elvira scratched her chin. "At the risk of not minding my own business, you and Pete have a will, right?"

"We do."

"Good, because it's best to have those things spelled out, especially when you have valuable assets," Elvira said. "Pete's stuff. Your stuff."

"What about you?" Carlita set her purse on the desk. "You have two businesses. The upstairs could be converted into rental units, not to mention you have your apartment."

"And the treasure Pete and I will find in his basement," Elvira added. "I'm working on updating mine as we speak."

"Leaving everything to me," Dernice said.

"Not quite. I want to make sure Zulilly is taken care of." Zulilly Fontaine, Elvira's only child, was in prison for killing her father's girlfriend. The last Carlita had heard, she was hoping to appeal her conviction.

To describe the mother/daughter relationship as strained was somewhat of an understatement. Still, Elvira loved Zulilly and clearly had concerns over what would happen to her if she died.

"Zu will be fine. I'll make sure she has a job if she gets out of prison," Dernice said. "Although I don't see her appeal going before a judge anytime soon."

"Me either." Elvira changed the subject. "How's it going with Cool Bones' investigation?"

Carlita tipped her hand back and forth. "It's one step forward and two steps back. Rudy McCoy and his landlord, Mrs. Culpepper, both mentioned a man named Cray."

"Cray as in cray-cray?"

"What does that mean?"

Elvira twirled her finger next to her forehead. "It means crazy."

"I suppose it's possible. Rudy was afraid of him. Culpepper remembered hearing his name." She told them about the black sedan, the logo and tracing it back to the Brick District.

"Those are some swanky digs," Elvira said. "You can't make it past the gate without being a member."

"It is an impressive area with gorgeous estates, a country club, you name it," Carlita said. "I just left there."

"How did you get in?" Dernice asked.

"Tori Montgomery is a lifetime member."

"Ah." Elvira pressed the tips of her fingers together. "I should've known. Montgomery has more connections than anyone I've ever met."

"Unfortunately, we hit a dead-end when we tried to find out if this Cray person worked or works for the Brick District. The records are online, at least according to the manager we spoke with."

"But he wasn't about to let you take a look," Dernice guessed.

"Nope. However, he made a point of telling Tori and me the records were online, which leads me to believe there might be a way to view them, some sort of backdoor access."

Elvira drummed her fingers on the desk. "And you think I might be able to help?"

"I'm hoping so."

"It's gonna cost you. I can't work for free."

"I understand," Carlita said. "How much for a quick search?"

Elvira rattled off what sounded like a reasonable amount.

"I'll pay. How long will it take?"

"It depends on where the records are located." Elvira began humming under her breath, her fingers flying over the computer keys. "This is proving harder than I thought."

"You can't find the records?"

"Not yet. Maybe I'm going about it all wrong. I'm gonna try Kiveski's go-to."

"Boyfriend Sharky Kiveski?"

"Yeah. He's all over the dark web. He showed me a nifty trick."

Carlita leaned in, curious to see what she was talking about.

Elvira covered the screen with her hands. "You'll have to look away. It's top secret. I promised him I would never show anyone else how to access the site."

"Fine." Carlita looked away. "You are two peas in a pod."

"Like spaghetti and meatballs," Elvira sing-songed. "I'm in."

"Awesome."

"Don't start celebrating yet. I'm doing something wrong. I must've forgotten a step."

Dernice wandered over. She stood behind her sister, offering pointers. "Try the Orion System."

"Good idea. I forgot about Orion."

"I have to ask. What on earth is the Orion System?"

"It's a new, fast-as-wildfire internet system a lot of government agencies are switching to. There's less chance of being hacked and it's much more secure." Elvira went into a long and technical explanation about the pros and cons, most of which went over Carlita's head.

"I've already spent twenty bucks on accessing Sharky's dark website. The Orion System is gonna cost another thirty. Unfortunately, I'll need to pass the additional cost on to you."

"Fine. Whatever. What's thirty more dollars in the scheme of things?"

"If you're able to get Cool Bones out of this jam, he's going to owe you big time."

"You should've seen how depressed he was earlier when I visited him. To be perfectly honest, I think he's given up hope."

"If you do the crime, you should do the time," Dernice said.

"Cool Bones didn't do the crime," Carlita said. "He's innocent. The good news is Tori called Mayor Puckett, who pulled a few strings. Cool Bones will be free by the end of the day."

"It helps to have the right connections. I think I found it." Elvira grew quiet. "Wow. Yeah. Brick District has all kinds of files on Orion. What department are you looking for?"

"The driver's center."

"Man, this web is powerful," Elvira said. "I'm gonna have to mention it to Sharky so he can add it to his arsenal. You said the name you're looking for was Cray."

Carlita pulled her cell phone from her purse and clicked on the photo she'd taken of Cool Bones' bookie log. "It's spelled C-R-A-Y."

"Got it. You were on the right track. This guy worked for the Brick District as a driver years ago." Elvira printed off a single sheet and handed it to Carlita.

She slipped her reading glasses on. "Doug Cray McCoy. His last name is the same as the murdered guy."

"Stand by." Elvira reached for the mouse. She tapped the screen, making a clicking noise with her tongue.

"What are you doing?"

"Trying to confirm Rudy McCoy and Cray are related," Elvira said. "I'm gonna guess yes, but you never want to assume."

While Elvira searched, Carlita used her phone to pull up the address listed as the last known for Cray. It was in a less-than-desirable part of town, but not necessarily in the worst area.

"I'm not finding a connection," Elvira finally said. "Which means I can't confirm the deceased and this Cray person are related."

Dernice scooted closer to Carlita, studying the paper. "This is over by Gleason Street, close to where Rudy McCoy lived."

"You're right," Carlita said excitedly. "They're definitely within walking distance."

"Which means if Cray was the killer, he could have easily sneaked over to the apartment, killed McCoy and left undetected."

"If Cray lived there at the time of the murder. You said Eunice Culpepper mentioned seeing a Brick District sedan in the neighborhood multiple times," Elvira said. "Which brings up another point. If Doug Cray McCoy and Rudy McCoy were related, wouldn't the snoopy landlady know this?"

"I'm not sure," Carlita said. "Maybe they were distant relatives."

"Or maybe he made a point of keeping their relationship a secret. This Rudy guy introduced his relative to the bookie business, and he stabbed him in the back by stealing Rudy's accounts."

"Like Rudy did to Cool Bones," Carlita interrupted. "Rudy found out. They argued, and in a fit of rage, Cray murdered him."

"The only way to find out for sure is to track down Doug Cray McCoy," Carlita said.

"Gleason Street runs all the way across town," Dernice said. "If I remember correctly, this address is in a rough area."

Carlita folded the paper in thirds. "Thank you for the information. Send me a bill and I'll pay it."

"Online," Elvira said. "If you pay online, I offer a five percent discount."

"Fine. I'll pay it online."

"But not with a credit card. You'll need to use a debit card. Otherwise I'll have to tack on the bank's ridiculous fee." Elvira shoved her chair back, scurrying after Carlita, who was heading to the door. "You might want to take Tony with you."

"I would rather not involve him. He has enough on his plate right now." Carlita grasped the door handle. "I have the perfect person in mind, someone who has no qualms about scoping out sketchy neighborhoods. And since I'm here, you can tell me where to find him, so I can give him a call to see if he has time to help."

Chapter 27

With information about a possible location for the elusive "Cray" in hand and a promise of help from Luigi, Carlita returned home. She found Rambo snoozing by the slider. He scrambled to his feet and trotted over. "You wanna go for a ride?"

After a quick break to freshen up, she and her pup hit the road. Carlita took the main drag out of town toward the highway. Only a few miles in, her directional app alerted her she'd reached the destination.

She steered her car into the *Savannah Cycles* parking lot. Clusters of red, white and blue balloons were tied to the handles of shiny black motorcycles. A large red and white tent covered an entire section of the property.

Men clad in black leather jackets and leather boots stood next to women, sporting sleeveless jackets with boho bandanas tied around their heads.

Womp...womp, womp, womp. Loud music blared from a tower of speakers. A clown on stilts clomped past.

An employee wearing a *Savannah Cycles* nametag flagged her down.

Carlita lowered her driver's side window.

"Welcome to Savannah Cycles Bikefest. Public parking is over there." He jabbed his finger toward a packed parking lot directly behind a row of shiny black choppers.

"I'm here to pick up a friend, Luigi Baruzzo. He works for EC Security Services."

"Luigi? I saw him over by the concession stand."

"Thanks." Carlita crept toward her destination. She finally spotted Luigi seated atop a motorcycle, a cigarette dangling from his mouth while he chatted with a group of bikers.

He caught her eye and sauntered over. "Hey, Mrs. T. You ready to roll?"

"As ready as I'll ever be." She waited for him to climb in the car. "For a minute, I thought I was at the circus."

"I'm not sure what's up with the clowns." Luigi shrugged. "I guess someone thought it would bring in the bikers."

"If hiring clowns was the plan, it worked. This place is packed."

"You should've seen it earlier. It's the biggest motorcycle event in Georgia," Luigi said. "Dernice is kinda bummed. She wanted to do the gig but had already promised to work undercover for Elvira."

Carlita shot her passenger a side glance. "Work undercover doing what?"

"Unfortunately, I'm not allowed to talk about it." Luigi patted Rambo's head and tossed his work hat on the backseat. "She's handling a sensitive investigation and needed boots on the ground. I can tell you it's a high-profile public figure."

"She better watch whose toes she's stepping on."

"I already warned her, but the money is good and she didn't want to turn it down. She's trying to earn some extra cash for her Alaska trip."

"I keep forgetting she's leaving."

"It's all she's talking about. That and kicking Pete's excavation project up a notch."

"She's already pushed for more access." Carlita tapped the brakes to let a juggling clown cross the parking lot before continuing. "Thank you for tagging along today. Elvira seemed a smidgen concerned about me scoping out the area alone."

"For good reason. I'm no sissy, but you wouldn't catch me over there alone at night." Luigi shared a story about a co-worker who was lured to the neighborhood, only to be robbed at gunpoint and beaten. "He ended up having his finger amputated."

Carlita grimaced. "Poor guy. It sounds rough."

Luigi patted his pocket. "I have my Sig loaded and ready to protect."

"The plan is to get in and out as quickly as possible. With any luck, we'll finally be able to locate Cray...Doug McCoy, a man I think may know something about Rudy McCoy's death."

"Same last name?" Luigi asked. "They're related?"

"I haven't confirmed it, but it's reasonable to assume they could be." Carlita's cell phone rang, a ring tone she immediately recognized. "I better take this call." She tapped the answer button. "Hey, Mercedes."

"Hey, Ma. Where are you?"

"With Luigi. We have a lead on Cray, whose real name is Doug McCoy."

"McCoy. The guy has the same last name as the dead man?"

"Yes. Elvira tracked down an address for me. She couldn't tell if they were related. Luigi and I are on our way over there to check it out and hopefully talk to him."

"The reason I'm calling is I have a surprise for you. Swing by the apartment when you're done."

"What is it?"

"You'll have to wait and see."

"We should be there in about half an hour, tops."

"We'll be waiting."

Carlita reached the intersection leading into town and turned left. With a few more turns, they reached their destination.

Compact block homes were sandwiched in between traditional brownstones. Unkempt yards and cracked sidewalks led to sloping steps. Porches in various states of disrepair was the theme of the neighborhood.

Nearly half of the windows were boarded up. Carlita noticed a tattered curtain move. "We're being watched."

"I bet. Mind if I have a smoke?"

"Be my guest, as long as the smoke blows out." Luigi rolled the window down and lit a cigarette. "This ain't as rough as the South Bronx."

"I don't think any area is as rough as the Bronx." Carlita eased her car alongside the curb and shifted into park in front of a small brick bungalow. "This is it."

"It's a dump," Luigi said bluntly.

A man on a bike pedaled past, slowing when he noticed Carlita and Luigi sitting inside the car. For a second, she thought he was going to stop. Instead, he kept going.

"Now what?" Luigi asked. "We sit and wait to see if someone shows up?"

"Or we go ring the doorbell."

"I vote for ringing the bell." Luigi took a final drag off his cigarette and flicked the butt out the window. "Lock yourself in."

An uneasy feeling settled over Carlita. "I'm beginning to think this wasn't such a great idea."

"It'll be fine." Luigi swung the door open. "I got a million excuses and a good reason for a sales pitch."

"Be careful." As soon as Luigi slammed the door, Carlita clicked the door locks.

She held her breath, watching through the front windshield as he casually strolled down the sidewalk and climbed the steps. He rapped on the door and waited.

Nothing happened.

He did a full one-eighty, scoping out the neighborhood, before trying again. Finally, the door opened. A man, balding and a good six inches shorter than Luigi, joined him on the porch.

Carlita slid down in the seat. With cell phone in hand, she aimed it in their direction and pressed the "record" button. She could see them talking over the tippy top of the steering wheel.

Shaking his head, the man turned to head back inside.

Luigi stopped him. He patted his pockets and handed him something before making his way back to the car.

Carlita unlocked the doors. "What happened?"

"I offered Elvira's security services and gave him my card," Luigi said. "He told me it was a no-solicitation neighborhood. I apologized and asked for his name. He told me it was Joe Blow."

"So...if it was Cray McCoy, he didn't want to give you his name."

"Nope. I got a good look at him," Luigi said.

"And I got a good video of him."

"Look at you?" Luigi playfully punched her in the arm. "Being all investigative and professional-like."

"I would've made Elvira proud." Carlita started the car and pulled away from the curb.

"Joe Blow" stood on his porch, watching as they drove off. "Something tells me he doesn't like people coming to his door."

They reached the stop sign and turned right toward home. Although only a few blocks away, Walton Square was like a different world. Tidy, clean, orderly and safe, at least for the most part.

"Mercedes asked me to stop by." Carlita parked in the lot at the far end. Falling into step, she and Luigi, with Rambo taking the lead, strolled toward the apartment.

Mercedes stood waiting for them on the stoop. She wasn't alone.

Carlita let out a loud whoop. "Now this is a sight for sore eyes."

Chapter 28

Carlita jogged to the other end of the alley. "You're free!"

"Free as a bird, at least for now." Cool Bones beamed. "Tori Montgomery worked her magic."

"She sure did." Carlita took a step back, noting the dark circles under her friend's eyes and worry lines creasing his forehead. "You look like you could use some rest."

"Rest, a shower, clean clothes, a decent meal."

Luigi caught up with them. He gave his friend and neighbor a congratulatory slap on the back. "It's good to see you."

"It's good to be home."

"What happened?" Carlita asked.

"I was sitting on my cot, right after they finished serving lunch. A guard came to the cell and called me out. Next thing I know, he's escorting me to the judge's chambers. I figured this was it. He was gonna throw the book at me." Cool Bones' lower lip trembled as he struggled to maintain his composure. "He said the mayor had asked for my release. I paid the bond and here I am."

"Tori and Mayor Puckett are friends. When she found out you were in jail, she started making some calls, trying to get you out."

"I'm going upstairs right now to call and thank her." Cool Bones reached for the doorknob.

Carlita stopped him. "Before you go, Elvira did some digging around. Luigi and I think we may have found Cray, also known as Doug McCoy."

Cool Bones stared at Carlita. "The mystery man, Cray, is related to Rudy McCoy?"

"Elvira wasn't able to confirm it. She tracked down an address for Cray. It's not far from Gleason Street."

Luigi picked up. "So Carlita and I went over there. I knocked on the door. A guy finally answered. I offered Elvira's security services. He declined. I asked for his name and he told me it was Joe Blow."

"Meaning none of your business," Cool Bones said. "What did he look like?"

"I'm glad you asked." Carlita tapped her pocket. "Why don't you go ahead and give Tori a call? After you're done, we'll show you the video I recorded."

"Sounds good. I need to get my name cleared as soon as possible." Cool Bones told her the Thirsty Crow had removed him and his band from their entertainment schedule. "All our upcoming gigs have been cancelled. My guys need to put food on the table and keep a roof over their heads."

"Including you," Carlita said. "I'm sorry to hear this."

"Hey." Elvira emerged from her building and sprinted across the alley. "Tori got you out?"

"She sure did," Cool Bones said. "I was getting ready to give her a call to thank her."

Elvira tapped Carlita's arm. "Have you had a chance to check out Cray McCoy's place yet?"

"Yeah. Luigi knocked on the door. A man answered, but wouldn't give Luigi his name. I recorded the whole thing," Carlita said. "We're going to have Cool Bones take a look at it to see if he recognizes the guy."

"Channel 2 news released a special segment about McCoy's death. They have photos, witnesses...the whole shebang. I was thinking Cool Bones might want to check it out." Elvira tapped the side of her forehead. "Maybe it will jog his memory."

"We should all check it out," Carlita said. "Are they running it again?"

"It doesn't matter. We can watch it online."

"But first, I have a very important person I need to thank." Cool Bones slipped inside the apartment. He returned a short time later, his favorite fedora perched atop his head, looking more relaxed than Carlita had seen him in days. "I'm ready to take a look at what you have."

The group assembled upstairs in Mercedes' apartment. Carlita forwarded the video recording to her daughter's email. She promptly logged on and cast it to her living room television.

Luigi appeared, standing on the man's porch. He knocked, looked around and knocked a second time. Finally, a man emerged. He slipped out of the brick bungalow and closed the door behind him.

"This is where I'm offering security services," Luigi said. "He was telling me to leave, and I handed him a business card."

Cool Bones stepped directly in front of the television. "I don't believe it."

"Believe what?" Carlita asked.

317

"What I'm seeing. It's him."

"Him who?"

"Rudy McCoy. The man right there is Rudy McCoy," Cool Bones said.

The room grew quiet, so quiet you could hear a pin drop.

Elvira was the first to speak. "It's been years since you last saw the guy. How can you be certain it's him?"

"Because of the scar on the back of his neck, right below his hairline." Cool Bones motioned to Mercedes. "Can you rewind it and stop where he turns around?"

"You bet." She did as he requested, pausing the recording when the man turned.

Cool Bones tapped the television screen. "Right there. He's got the scar."

Carlita made a timeout with her hands. "What you're saying is the man who answered the door is the same guy you're accused of murdering?"

"One hundred percent."

"If this is Rudy McCoy, whose body is in his coffin?" Elvira asked.

Carlita's mind whirled as she struggled to put the pieces together.

"We need to figure this out." Mercedes paced. "Let's start with the theory Rudy McCoy and Cray, aka Doug McCoy, are related."

"Maybe a relative, a twin, or someone with a striking resemblance," Elvira said.

"Correct. The dead man, found inside Rudy McCoy's apartment, was mistaken for Rudy. Meanwhile, the real Rudy McCoy vanishes."

"All the while he's living right down the street from where his murder supposedly took place," Cool Bones said. "How we gonna convince the cops this man is Rudy McCoy and figure out who is buried in Rudy's grave?"

"Sam," Mercedes said.

"Something tells me the key to solving this mystery is buried in the cemetery," Carlita said.

"Sam should be home any minute now. I'll ask him if he can reach out to someone at the department, someone willing to listen to us."

While they waited, Cool Bones watched the video again. "This is the guy. I'll bet my life this is Rudy McCoy."

"Don't forget about the Channel 2 news program," Elvira said.

Mercedes tracked down the updated report and cast it to the television. The fifteen-minute segment gave the history of the case. The reporter played Eunice Culpepper's interview. There were photos of Rudy McCoy and even a still photo of the apartment building.

Although the reporter didn't give Cool Bones' name, she told viewers the authorities had arrested a person believed to have been behind the murder.

"They must have missed the memo I'm out of jail," Cool Bones said.

The special ended with the reporter standing next to Rudy's headstone.

Carlita placed a light hand on the back of her neck, staring thoughtfully at the image. "We need help."

"Sam should be here any second." Mercedes ran into the hall, returning moments later with her boyfriend.

Taking turns, they brought him up to speed on what had transpired.

"The bottom line is, we need a more thorough investigation to figure out who is buried in Rudy McCoy's grave," Carlita summarized.

Sam left, but not before promising he would see what he could do.

"Elvira is pretty good at digging holes," Luigi joked. "Give her a shovel and pickax and she'll have the coffin out of the ground before you can say biscuits and graves."

"I would have it up, out, and back in the ground by daybreak," she boasted.

Carlita wagged her finger. "Don't you dare. We need to do this lawfully and legally."

"Unless you're up for more community service," Mercedes said.

"No thanks. Picking up trash is a one and done for this chick."

Sam returned a short time later. "I was able to reach Detective Polivich. He knows the person who is handling the case. He agreed to swing by and hear what you have to say."

"Thank you, Sam." Mercedes bounced on the tips of her toes and kissed his cheek.

"You're welcome. Cool Bones is my friend, too."

While they waited, they shared theories about how Rudy McCoy had managed to hide his identity for all these years, pretending to be dead.

Hopefully, Polivich would be willing to not only listen, but act. If not, a dead man would continue living his life while an innocent man spent the rest of *his* behind bars.

Chapter 29

Detective Polivich quietly listened while Carlita, Mercedes and Cool Bones laid out their case. "Investigators have already exhumed Mr. McCoy's body and examined his remains."

"We showed you the video," Carlita said. "Cool Bones recognizes the scar on the back of this man's neck. This is Rudy McCoy. If McCoy is alive, who is buried in his grave?"

"You state a strong case." The detective shifted his feet. "Let me run it by the lead investigator to get his thoughts."

"If not, we could contact the local news channel to share Cool Bones' side of the story," Elvira said. "I don't think the local police department wants to be viewed as inept or incompetent."

"I'm not gonna go down without a fight," Cool Bones vowed. "I'm telling you...the man who answered the door is Rudy McCoy. Whether he had a twin who is buried or a relative with an eerie resemblance is something the police need to figure out."

The detective jotted down Cool Bones' cell phone number and promised he would see what he could do.

Carlita escorted him to the alley and returned. "Well?"

"We wait," Sam said.

"And if the cops won't do anything." Elvira made a digging motion. "We dig."

"I appreciate all the help. If you don't mind, I would like to head home and take a long, hot shower." Cool Bones thanked them for their support and promised to let them know if Polivich contacted him before he left.

Elvira glanced at her watch. "I'm heading home to take a nap, so I'm well rested. We'll need to do our digging after dark."

Carlita briefly closed her eyes. "You can't be serious."

"If the cops won't help, what choice do we have?" Elvira stepped into the hall. "Call me when you get word."

"Ditto for me," Sam said. "I don't think the police department wants a story airing about how they potentially screwed up a highly publicized murder case."

Luigi took off, leaving Carlita and Mercedes alone.

"Maybe I should whip up another batch of biscuits and gravy and run it down to the police department," Carlita offered.

"I don't think it will be necessary...at least I hope not." Mercedes flopped down on the sofa. "The lead investigator could decide our case isn't worth the hassle, which means Elvira's grave digging idea might not be as far out there as it seems. Your cell phone is ringing, Ma."

Carlita tracked down her purse and discovered she'd missed a call from Pete. "Where are you?"

"At Mercedes' place. I'm on my way home."

"I'm free for the rest of the evening and was wondering if I could meet you for a delicious Italian dinner," Pete enticed.

"Do you have somewhere specific in mind?" Carlita chuckled.

"As a matter of fact, I do. Why don't you save us a romantic table for two at my favorite Italian restaurant? I'll be there in a flash," he promised.

"You have yourself a deal...a date." Carlita told him goodbye and slid her phone into her purse. "I'm meeting Pete for dinner over at the restaurant."

"How romantic," Mercedes sighed. "Pete's a good guy."

"The best." Carlita gathered her things and made the quick trip down the alley. Entering through the front door, she asked the hostess for a table in the corner. It was early evening, which meant a few coveted quiet spots were still available. While she waited, she ordered drinks.

Pete arrived moments later. He caught her eye and strode through the restaurant, a bouquet of pink carnations and yellow roses in hand.

"Dinner and flowers?" Carlita slipped out of her chair and greeted him with a kiss.

"You mentioned Sam buying Mercedes flowers. It reminded me you were long overdue." He set the bouquet on the table. "I figured something positive would be nice for a change."

"I have good news. Cool Bones is out of jail." Carlita filled him in on what had transpired. Meeting Tori, visiting the Brick District, chatting with the manager, visiting Doug "Cray" McCoy's last known address. "Cool Bones swears the guy Luigi talked to was none other than the dead man."

"No kidding. I'm sure the authorities will be very interested."

"I hope so. Sam convinced Detective Polivich to stop by and let us lay out our case. I think he's going to try to help."

"By doing what?"

"Figuring out who is buried in Rudy McCoy's grave. I'm sure the investigators will also be interested in finding out who lives in Doug McCoy's house," Carlita said.

"Wouldn't that be something if McCoy killed a family member and somehow made it appear to be him? All the while, he's free as a bird, living his life as someone else," Pete mused.

"I'm beginning to believe this is what happened. Now, all we need is proof."

"I'm surprised Elvira hasn't volunteered to do the digging."

"She's home taking a nap in the off chance her services are needed."

"The woman never stops."

"Never." Carlita reached for the menu. "And on that note, I'm starving."

The couple enjoyed a leisurely dinner, talking about work, their businesses and the excavation project. Near the end of the meal, her phone rang. It was Cool Bones.

"Hey, Carlita. Did I catch you at a bad time?"

"Not at all. Pete and I are at Ravello's finishing our dinner."

"I have some great news." He told her the investigators were reluctant to take another look at McCoy's remains until finding out he planned to contact the local news stations. "After they found out, they said they would return to the cemetery."

"When?" she asked.

"Tonight. I wanna be there."

"Me too," Carlita said. "Did they give you a time?"

"Sure did. Dusk."

"Pete and I will go with you." Carlita told him they would swing by to pick him up before sending a group text to Sam, Mercedes, Luigi, and Elvira, filling them in.

The texts flew back and forth, fast and furious...everyone wanting to be on hand to see exactly what the authorities found.

At six fifty-seven on the dot, the couple pulled into the alley and found Cool Bones, Mercedes and Sam already there waiting.

Elvira and her crew sat idling in an EC Investigative Services van. Loaded up and ready to roll, the vehicles caravanned across town to the cemetery.

They arrived to find several police cars along with a white crime scene van parked off to the side.

"I brought some flashlights." Elvira handed them out. "We're going to want to hang back and steer clear of the activity."

"I hope you're telling yourself that," Carlita said.

"Or she can grab a shovel and offer to help," Sam teased.

"I might." Elvira craned her neck. "I see them over there."

Walking single file with Cool Bones in the lead, Carlita and the others took the main path to the back of the cemetery.

A group of workers stood near the gravesite Carlita recognized as Rudy McCoy's. Although they were several yards away, Carlita knew the exact moment they unearthed the coffin.

She held her breath, watching as the work crew lifted it out of the ground. A man, one who appeared to be in charge, motioned for them to remove the lid.

"I can't stand it. I'm moving closer." Elvira tiptoed past several headstones, stopping only a few feet away from the now open casket.

Carlita trailed behind. "What are they saying?" she asked in a low voice.

"I don't know," Elvira whispered back.

Cool Bones caught up with them. "How's it going?"

"We're not sure. The investigators keep walking around, like they're looking for something." Carlita spotted a familiar figure. It was Detective Polivich.

He held up a hand, said something to a uniformed officer, and made his way over. "Mrs. Taylor."

"Hello again, Detective Polivich. We were told the investigators were planning to look into Cool Bones' claim about Rudy McCoy still being alive."

"Correct. They're exhuming the body to do some additional DNA testing," he said. "I thought you might be interested to know the police are on their way over to chat with whoever is living at his brother Doug's last known residence."

Carlita perked up. "His brother?"

"Yes. We've discovered Rudy McCoy had a brother, Doug McCoy, who lives at the address you visited earlier today."

"The man I know for a fact to be Rudy McCoy. Finally." Cool Bones clasped his hands, lifting his gaze toward the night sky. "Thank you, God. This nightmare is finally ending."

Chapter 30

"There's the man of the hour." Carlita led the round of enthusiastic applause. Cool Bones, with pep in his step, strolled into the courtyard. He pressed his hands over his heart and blew kisses to those who were there to celebrate his exoneration...free from the heavy cloud of conviction hanging over his head.

Pete, Mercedes, Sam, Elvira, Dernice, Luigi, Tony, a very pregnant Shelby, Violet, Steve Winters and his girlfriend Paisley...those who had worked hard to help free the innocent man.

"Speech...speech..." Mercedes chanted.

The crowd grew quiet.

"Thank you from the bottom of my heart for not giving up and proving my innocence. If not for all of you, working together to help figure out what happened to Rudy McCoy, I would not be standing here today."

Pete tapped his wife's shoulder. "All spearheaded by my stubborn wife, who refused to give up."

"Carlita was instrumental." Cool Bones motioned to his band, who were off to the side, setting up and getting ready to play. "I have some exciting news. The Thirsty Crow has put the Jazz Boys and me back on the schedule. All the gigs we had on the books are back in play, meaning me and my guys are once again in business."

Another round of enthusiastic applause ensued.

Cool Bones continued. "I spoke with Detective Polivich and have an update."

"I can't wait to hear the details about what exactly happened that day when Mrs. Culpepper witnessed your altercation with Rudy," Carlita said.

"That's where it gets interesting. According to her official statement, she saw me grab the bat from Rudy and knock him down. Culpepper thought she overheard me say, 'I'm gonna finish you and you can bet on that.' What I really said was, 'I'm finished with you and this bettin' business.'"

Cool Bones told them the investigators drove over to Doug "Cray" McCoy's last place of residence, the small bungalow Luigi and Carlita had visited. "Rudy and his brother Doug were both in the bookie business and began feuding over territory. Doug showed up at Rudy's place. They argued and Rudy killed his brother. In a panic, he staged the scene, making it look like he was the one who had died."

"And maybe even been the one who called police to stop by for a wellness check," Mercedes pointed out.

"Ah." Carlita arched her eyebrow. "You're right. I never thought about that."

"I'm guessing we've been waiting for additional DNA testing to prove Rudy wasn't the one buried in the grave," Elvira said.

"Yep. *Extensive* DNA testing confirmed the person buried in Rudy's grave was, in fact, his brother Doug McCoy." Cool Bones shifted his feet. "They never were able to find a murder weapon, only stating Doug McCoy died from blunt force trauma."

"I bet when he found out you had been picked up and charged with his murder, he couldn't believe his good fortune," Pete said.

Cool Bones folded his arms. "He thought he was in the clear, and he was until Carlita and Luigi showed up on his doorstep. He's going to be behind bars for a very long time for murdering his own flesh and blood."

"Which is right where he belongs." Carlita clapped her hands. "Dig in everyone. There's plenty of food."

Cool Bones and his band took their place on the makeshift stage after finishing their celebratory meal.

Music and laughter, food and friends. It was a night to remember, to celebrate the good guy winning.

Finally, the festivities began winding down, and guests started heading home. Carlita noticed Shelby seated off to the side, an anxious expression on her face. Tony hovered nearby. "Is everything okay?"

"Shelby is having contractions. It's time to head to the hospital."

"The baby is on the way." Carlita knelt next to Violet. "Do you want to stay with Nana until the baby gets here?"

"I want to be with Mommy and Daddy." Violet leaned against Tony, grasping his hand.

"It's all right." Shelby winced. "My aunt is already on her way to the hospital to meet us. Violet can hang out with her."

Carlita trailed behind the couple, who began making their way toward Tony's car. "Please call me as soon as you have news. I'll have my phone by my side."

"We will, Ma." While Tony helped Shelby into the car, Carlita ran upstairs to their apartment to grab the hospital bag.

She flew back down the steps, opened the rear car door and placed it on the seat next to Violet. "I'll be waiting for the call."

"You're first on the list," Tony promised.

Carlita whispered a small prayer as her son's car, with his family inside, sped off. Something told her it was going to be a long night.

*****

Carlita, with Pete by her side, clutched the bouquet of pink and blue balloons, covered in smiling teddy bears and grinning giraffes, making her way along the hospital's gleaming corridor. "I'm so excited."

"You sure you don't know if we have a new grandson or granddaughter?" Pete asked.

"No. Tony refused to give me even the tiniest hint. He wants us to be surprised."

"Hey!"

The couple turned to find Mercedes hurrying to catch up, carrying a similarly sized bouquet of balloons and a gift bag. "I thought that was you. It took me a few minutes to find a parking spot."

With a quick stop by the nurse's station to get the room number, the trio zigged and zagged until finally finding the door with the nameplate, "Garlucci."

Carlita gave it a light rap and stuck her head around the corner.

Proud Papa Tony sat next to Shelby's hospital bed. Violet stood on the other side, leaning against her mother's arm, a look of adoration etched on her face as she stared at the tiny newborn.

Carlita tiptoed closer, her heart melting. Perfect. Button nose. Chubby cheeks. Wisps of dark hair swirling on top of the baby's head.

She handed the balloons to her son. "The baby is beautiful," she whispered. "Welcome to the family."

Pete patted Tony's arm. "Congratulations. We have another Garlucci to call Savannah home."

"Absolutely." Tony gazed lovingly at his wife. "Shelby was a real trooper. I have to say, she made it look easy."

Shelby placed a gentle kiss on the baby's forehead. "Time to meet Nana, Poppa and Auntie Mercedes."

"Before I hold the baby." Carlita called Violet over and handed her a gift bag with red hearts and the words "Big Sister." "This is for you."

"A present for me?" Violet asked.

Carlita solemnly nodded. "Being a big sister is a special job. I know you're going to be the best one ever."

"I am. I will be very careful. If Mom or Dad need anything, I can go get it." Violet, with a look of devotion on her face, wrapped her small arm around Tony's waist and gazed up at him. "Daddy got me a special gift."

Tony affectionately ruffled his daughter's hair. "You want to show them?"

Violet tugged a delicate chain from her blouse. Hooked to the chain were four intertwined circles. "It has a circle for me, for Mommy, Daddy and the baby," she said proudly.

Carlita blinked back sudden tears and gave her a gentle hug. "I love you so much, Violet. You're such a good girl. Open your gift."

She reached into the bag and pulled out a floppy-eared bunny wearing a dandelion yellow "Big Sister" shirt. There was a "Big Sister Helper" book, along with several of Violet's favorite candies.

"Thank you, Nana. You're the best." Violet flung her arms around Carlita's neck and hugged her tightly.

Carlita swallowed hard, certain she had the most wonderful grandchildren on earth. "And you're the best granddaughter ever."

Tony took the baby from Shelby and passed the newborn to his mother. "The best granddaughters ever," he corrected. "Welcome Melody Carlita Garlucci."

The end.

The Series Continues!

Read Bungled Burglaries in Savannah

Join The Fun

Get Updates on New Releases, FREE and
Discounted eBooks, Giveaways, & More!

hopecallaghan.com

Read More by Hope

Made in Savannah Cozy Mystery Series

After the mysterious death of her mafia "made man" husband, Carlita Garlucci makes a shocking discovery. Follow the Garlucci family saga as Carlita and her daughter try to escape their NY mob ties and make a fresh start in Savannah, Georgia. They soon realize you can run but can't hide from your past.

Cruise Director Millie Mystery Series

Cruise Director Millie Mystery Series is the new spin-off series from the wildly popular Millie's Cruise Ship Cozy Mysteries.

Millie's Cruise Ship Cozy Mystery Series

Hoping for a fresh start after her recent divorce, sixty something Millie Sanders, lands her dream job as the assistant cruise director onboard the "Siren of the Seas." Too bad no one told her murder is on the itinerary.

Easton Island Mystery Series

Easton Island is the continuing saga of one woman's journey from incredible loss to finding a past she knew nothing about, including a family who both embraces and fears her and a charming island that draws her in. This inspirational women's fiction series is for lovers of family sagas, friendship, mysteries, and clean romance.

Lack of Luxury Series (Liz and the Garden Girls)

Green Acres meets the Golden Girls in this new cozy mystery spin-off series featuring Liz and the Garden Girls!

Garden Girls Cozy Mystery Series

A lonely widow finds new purpose for her life when she and her senior friends help solve a murder in their small Midwestern town.

Garden Girls - The Golden Years

The new spin-off series of the Garden Girls Mystery series! You'll enjoy the same fun-loving characters as they solve mysteries in the cozy town of Belhaven. Each book will focus on one of the Garden Girls as they enter their "golden years."

Divine Cozy Mystery Series

After relocating to the tiny town of Divine, Kansas, strange and mysterious things begin to happen to businesswoman, Jo Pepperdine and those around her.

Samantha Rite Mystery Series

Heartbroken after her recent divorce, a single mother is persuaded to book a cruise and soon finds herself caught in the middle of a deadly adventure. Will she make it out alive?

Sweet Southern Sleuths Short Stories Series

Twin sisters with completely opposite personalities become amateur sleuths when a dead body is discovered in their recently inherited home in Misery, Mississippi.

Meet Hope Callaghan

Hope Callaghan is an American mystery author who loves to write clean, fun-filled women's fiction mysteries with a touch of faith and romance. She is the author of more than 100 novels in ten different series.

Born and raised in a small town in West Michigan, she now lives in Florida with her husband. She is the proud mother of 3 wonderful children.

When she's not doing the thing she loves best - writing mysteries - she enjoys cooking, traveling and reading books.

Get a free cozy mystery ebook, new release alerts, and giveaways at hopecallaghan.com

Made-From-Scratch Biscuits & Gravy Recipe

<u>Biscuit Ingredients</u>:

2 cups all-purpose flour

1 tablespoon baking powder

1 teaspoon salt

⅓ cup butter, frozen and then grated with box grater

½ - 3/4 cup milk

<u>Directions</u>:

-Preheat oven to 450 degrees F (230 degrees C).

-In medium bowl, sift the flour, baking powder and salt.

-Use a pastry cutter or fork to cut butter into the flour mixture until crumbly.

-Gradually stir in the milk until the mixture pulls away from the sides of the bowl.

-Place dough on a floured surface.

-Knead 15-20 times.

-Press or roll dough until 1" thick.

-Use a large cutter or juice glass dipped in flour to cut the biscuits.

-Repeat until all dough is used.

-Place biscuits on ungreased baking sheet.

-Bake in preheated oven until edges turn brown – around 12 minutes.

Bacon Gravy Recipe

Ingredients:

½ cup crumbled bacon

¼ cup bacon drippings

¼ cup all-purpose flour

1 teaspoon salt, or to taste

1 teaspoon ground black pepper, or to taste

2 cups milk

¼ cup chopped scallion

1 sprig fresh rosemary

(Remove the leaves and mince)

Directions:

-Cook bacon in a large saucepan.

-Remove bacon from pan. Set aside.

-With the bacon drippings in the pan, reduce heat to simmer.

-Add flour, salt, and pepper to bacon drippings, stirring constantly.

-Add milk, ½ cup at a time.

-Crumble the fried bacon. Add to mixture.

-Add chopped scallion and minced fresh rosemary.

- Blend well.

-Remove from heat.

Serve over warm biscuits.

Made in the USA
Columbia, SC
02 May 2025

57474247R00214